MW00966862

ISBN 978-1-333-48334-0
PIBN 10510131

1 MONTH OF
FREE
READING

at

www.ForgottenBooks.com

By purchasing this book you are eligible for one month membership to ForgottenBooks.com, giving you unlimited access to our entire collection of over 700,000 titles via our web site and mobile apps.

To claim your free month visit:

www.forgottenbooks.com/free510131

English
Français
Deutsche
Italiano
Español
Português

www.forgottenbooks.com

Mythology Photography **Fiction**
Fishing Christianity **Art** Cooking
Essays Buddhism Freemasonry
Medicine **Biology** Music **Ancient
Egypt** Evolution Carpentry Physics
Dance Geology **Mathematics** Fitness
Shakespeare **Folklore** Yoga Marketing
Confidence Immortality Biographies
Poetry **Psychology** Witchcraft
Electronics Chemistry History **Law**
Accounting **Philosophy** Anthropology
Alchemy Drama Quantum Mechanics
Atheism Sexual Health **Ancient History**
Entrepreneurship Languages Sport
Paleontology Needlework Islam
Metaphysics Investment Archaeology
Parenting Statistics Criminology
Motivational

DUNSTER CASTLE,

AN

HISTORICAL

ROMANCE OF THE GREAT REBELLION.

BY

I. T. HEWLETT, M. A.

LATE OF WORCESTER COLLEGE, OXFORD.

————

IN THREE VOLUMES.

VOL. I.

LONDON:

HENRY COLBURN, PUBLISHER,

GREAT MARLBOROUGH STREET.

1846.

J. D. SMITH & CO, PRINTERS
7, EAST HARDING STREET, GOUGH SQUARE.

CHAPTER I.

ABOUT six o'clock in the morning of a brilliant May-day, 200 years ago, a small vessel of about ten tons burthen, rigged with two large lug-sails and a jib, might have been seen leaving the little port of Minehead, on the coast of Somerset, in the Bristol Channel. The morning was so calm that the wind, which ought to have *blown* from the north-east, scarcely served to lift the boat's little pendant from the mast against which it lay. The sails flapped lazily to and fro, as she rocked on the receding tide and was slowly carried beyond the little pier by the current.

The harbour-master, who stood at the pier-head,

watching the departure of the Blossom of Minehead, as the boat was called, placed his hands to
his mouth to form a speaking trumpet, and shouted
to the crew to "out sweeps and pull lustily into
the main tide." No further answer was returned
to him for his unasked advice, than a loud "Ay,
ay, sir," which came distinctly to his ear. The
oars remained beside the gunwales, and the crew
seemed contented to leave their boat to the gui-
dance of the stream. The captain, who stood at
the helm, rested his back against the tiller, so as to
bring her head round to the westward, filled his pipe,
and lighted it with a flint, which he struck against
the blade of a knife suspended round his neck by a
lanyard. The crew, who consisted of another
man apparently about the age of the captain, and a
tall stripling, who might have seen some seventeen summers, threw themselves upon the half-
deck in the fore part of the vessel, making a pillow
for their heads of the warps which had been hauled
in and coiled up when they left the pier-side.

"Lazy dogs, lazy dogs, I wot," said the harbour-
master as if soliloquizing, "but Giles Tudball was

ever willing to take things easy, and Will Bowering and the young springald seem well enough
inclined to follow his example. If the wind do
not spring up, and they be too idle to use their
sweeps, I doubt not but they will not have doubled the foreland ere tide be turned."

"Doubled the foreland, old boy," shouted a
gruff voice so close to the harbour-master's ear,
that, though he knew its owner was behind him, it
made him spring up from the pier-wall on which
he was resting his elbows—" Why should Giles
Tudball wish the little lively Blossom of Minyead
to double the foreland on a day like this?"

" The Blossom of Minyead (for so its inhabit-
ants of those days pronounced Minehead, by cor-
ruption probably of its ancient name Mynneved,)
I trow, Master Jenkins, goeth to Ly'mouth after
her usual freight, and, if her owner useth no more
exertion than he seems disposed to do just now,
the farmers must wait long for the lime-stone
that is to be burned in our kilns to manure their
lands."

"'Vast there old boy, and don't try to impose

upon a simple Welshman who knows but little,
yet enough to tell you that such mere cockle-
shells as that yonder go not after lime-stone at
all, and especially to Ly'mouth, but to Uphill,
opposite the Steep Holmes, on your side of the
water, or the more convenient and valuable cliffs
over right us in Wales," said Master Jenkins
rather indignantly.

" Said I lime-stone? Ly'mouth lime-stone,
Master Jenkins, and to thee? well, well, I grow
old and foolish, and you must have known that
when I said lime-stone, I meant Porlock whi-
tings which are caught with the hook, opposite
the little village of Linton. They are valuable,
Master Jenkins, and fetch much money of those
who love delicacies. Giles Tudball, you know, doth
little else but fish, though he may sometimes run
over to your side of the Channel and bring back,
in exchange for our broad cloths, a cargo of your
woollen yarns for the clothiers of Dunster."

" Little else, indeed," said Master Jenkins, "except it be, as some folks pretend, that he lies now
and then off the mouth of the Channel, near Lundy

Island, and lightens some of the ships from the Americas of a part of their cargoes, that they may float the lighter to the port of Bristol; or inter-changes civilities and strong waters for English gold with the Hollanders and the Frenchmen, who regard not our customs and laws."

"All scandal, sheer scandal, Master Jenkins; besides, an he did lay in a small store of tobaccoes and strong waters for his own use, doth he not pay tonnage and poundage and his share of the ship-tax as a freeholder of Minyead? answer me that!" said the harbour-master.

"Confound the tonnage and the poundage, and him that imposed so grievous a tax upon us!" said Master Jenkins.

"Nay, nay, speak not evil of King Charles, Master Jenkins; he must have money for his necessities; and thou know'st 'tis said the Parliament will grant him no further supplies, until he doth away with the bishops, and converts all the churches into meeting-houses."

"And let him do so, what care I? The parsons may burn their surplices, put on the black gown, and crop their heads as closely as Master George Browne, the late clerk of Dunster hath done, provided I have not to pay on both sides of the Channel for every cargo I run out and in with," said Master Jenkins.

"Be not wroth, be not wroth ; your good town of Cardiff flourisheth in despite of the King's taxes ; and Master Jenkins, sole owner and captain of the good cutter the St. David, can very well afford to pay the tonnage and poundage dues at every port he puts into."

Master Jenkins seemed inclined to argue the point, but the old harbour-master stopped his angry reply and continued—

"But as touching Giles Tudball and the tobaccoes and the strong waters: you know a sailor needs something to cheer him in wet and storm, stronger than Somersetshire cider or Welsh ales. If report speak not falsely, Hollands gin and the Virginian plant may be found among the stores of the St. David of Cardiff. Her captain is said to love his pipe and his glass as well as—"

"Master Luckes, the harbour-master of the

Port of Minyead; who, folk will say, keeps not his eyes so open as they might be, if they were not filled with rheum from the smoke-reek and the fumes of strong waters. He winks, it is said, somewhat frequently at a breach of the customs' laws."

" I am not of the customs, Master Jenkins, I have nought to do with their laws. I have my duties to perform, as master of this port and collector of all her dues, and I will take care that none, not even the owner and· captain of the St. David, escape by false guagings and short reckonings," replied Master Luckes in a great passion, and wending his way towards his official residence, at the foot of the pier which joins the lower town, and is situated close to the base of a high and steep hill, called Greenaleigh.

Master Jenkins smiled at the old man's wrath, but kept close to his side, throwing in a word or two as he walked along, to irritate him the more; for it was a favourite amusement with most of the seamen who put into Minehead, to excite the old harbour-master as much as they could, in order to see how suddenly his anger could be changed to placidity, and his forgiveness be obtained by an offer of his favourite liquor, Hollands gin, and materials for supplying his pipe.

" It is false, all false, Master Jenkins, you say it but to provoke me, but I will not be provoked : I am calm, skipper, quite calm, but may I be—"

" Hush, hush, 'vast there, Master Luckes," said the captain, holding up his hand deprecatingly.

" Nay, may I suffer more than devils are said to suffer, if I do not look *you* up sharp, your register must be set right, Master Jenkins, and your tonnage and poundage raised. I have been lenient, too lenient; but may I be—"

"Snugly seated in the little parlour of ' the Ship-aground,' with a glass of something warm, sweet, and strong before you, and a pipe of prime Virginia, such as Sir Walter Raleigh loved, and good King Jamie hated and abused, eh ? that was what you would have said, was it not? and so you shall, harbour-master; I have not yet broken my fast, and the host of the Ship-aground, your worthy son, Master Richard, hath a cold chine of Porlock mutton, which will serve us both ; and thou knowest that

Giles Tudball takes care that his corner cup-board lacks not the spirits or the weed. So come man, be not angry; I only joked with thee," said Master Jenkins holding out his tarry hand.

"Oh, an hast only been joking me all this time? ah! ah! well truly I thought so, and only feigned to be angry you see, so there is mine hand; and we will explore son Richard's pantry and taste what he hath in his buffet, but it is not contra-band, the duties have been paid," said the old man, winking at his companion, and hurrying as fast as his old limbs would allow him towards his son's hostelry.

"'Vast mate, avast, ere we enter Master Rich-ard's house, I would fain take another look at Giles Tudball and his craft: see, he is out in the run of the tide, and his sails catch the slight breeze that comes off down Channel. He will not be long ere he doubles Bossington Point, and runs safely into Culbone Cove."

"And why should he run into Culbone Cove of all places?" said the harbour-master, "you know that Culbone boasteth but of three little huts and

the smallest church in England, though I have
heard some of our sailors, who have visited the
Isle of Wight, say that they have seen one there
even smaller, dedicated to St. Lawrence, but I
doubt them Master Jenkins; they only say it to
annoy us: why, I ask thee then, should the Blossom
of Minyead make for Culbone? answer me that."

"Nay, Master Luckes, you need not be told
that Kitnore church is dedicated to St. Culbone,
though, who he was, it would puzzle a wiser head
than mine to tell thee, and that from him the
village hath its name.   This day, the first of May,
is the festival of St. Philip and St. James, and
on it is held Kitnore or Culbone revel, under the
license of the Bachells of Ashley-Combe, who
furnish the parson to the parish, and hold the
manor with its rights."

" Would'st hint, Master Jenkins, that the
Esquire of Ashley-Combe would license a revel, a
thing forbidden by the Parliament under heavy
penalties? or that Giles Tudball would risk his
good name, and waste his time at unlawful junketings and ale-meetings?"

" As to the license of the good Master Bachell of Ashley-Combe, I say nought about it, but you know, harbour-master, better than I can tell you, that Giles Tudball hath stowed away beneath his half-deck sundry yards of canvass, to form a tent or drinking-booth on Culbone-green, with certain barrels of beer and cider, not to recount other articles for good cheer, out of which¯ he expects to reap no small advantage to himself and your son Richard, who hath furnished him with the articles: neither hath he forgotten to take quoits, throwing-bars, and basket-sticks, for the recreation of such as love the sports of Englishmen, which Master Pym and his canting friends would fain put down, as wicked and abominable and savouring of prelacy and popery; though they were proclaimed to be lawful, even on the sabbath, by King James himself."

" Times are changed, times are changed, Master Jenkins;" said the old man, shaking his head mournfully, " men talk not as they were wont to talk, but speak the language of prophets and seers; such as we used to hear only in our churches. Sacred words be now used on most profane occasions, yet there is more roguery than ever in the world, and they that set up for the greatest share of piety are found to have the lightest weights and the shortest measures."

"I am no Papist, but boast myself to be a sound though an unworthy churchman, and yet can I not see that our revels, if they be well conducted, under the eyes of the nobles and gentry, as they have hitherto been, can be offensive either to God or man."

" Right, Master Jenkins, right, better play in sport, than do mischief in earnest. The poor man cannot always work, and, when not at work, he had better play than do worse; you know the old saying, ' idleness is the root of evil,' by which, I trow, is meant that, if a man be not at work or play, he is sure to be in mischief. I would rather that Laud, he that was Bishop of Bath, and is now of Canterbury, though he sees little of his see, seeing that he is in the Tower o' London, were left to lord it over us, than we should be as we are, in the hands of canting make-believes, who put a stop to all our games and sports; but how know you, Master Jenkins, that Giles Tudball hath a design to go to Culbone revel?"

"Tush, man!" replied the captain of the St. David, smiling, "you are grown old and silly and suspicious withal. Was I not with thee at son Richard's last even, until the smoke and the fumes of strong waters made you talk thick, and close your eyes, and finally obliged you to be put to bed? nay, never wince man, age will creep on, and the stomach and brain will fail a man at last, though he has been an honest toper in his time."

"Say no more, say no more, I confess I was overcome, and yet I did not drink deep," said the harbour-master.

"Not so deep as you were wont of yore certainly, but still sufficiently deep for an old man, and you slept sound enough to allow every vessel in port to discharge her cargo, without paying tonnage and poundage, had their owners been so disposed," said Master Jenkins.

"Nay, even you, Welshman though you be,

would not have suffered a good-natured old man to be wronged.   You would have roused me, you would have roused me, Master Jenkins."

" It might have been a difficult matter, more difficult than you are aware of; you heard us not as we carried the cargo to the Blossom of Minyead, though our barrows clattered close under your window."

"Did Giles Tudball then make known to you his intention of going to Culbone revel?"

" Ay did he, and I helped him and your son Richard to put everything on board, and am going over to join him by and by in my boat, with Alloway the butcher, and some other good wrestlers from the upper town, and am to have provender and free approach to the ale can for my trouble."

" And do you know who is gone with Giles Tudball and his mate Will Bowering? did they tell thee that?" said the old man looking earnestly in the captain's face.

" Ay man, they told me all, for they know that I may be trusted: besides, I have seen the young Hugh de Mohun before to-day, and even

carried him across to Cardiff in my vessel. He
is wild, and of a roving disposition, and ought
to be a sailor, for he loves the sea, and the more
stormy it is, the better he loves it."

" The Mohuns once, I am told, owned Dunster
Castle; is this young springald, think you, one of
the family?"

" Nay, I know not; I only know that he has
been for more than twelve months at Dunster, studying the humanities with good Master Snelling
the curate, who hath been placed over the church
in the room of Master Robert Browne, who, like
his father before him, hath become an Independent
and calls the Church, whose bread he ate of,
Antichrist; and has otherwise offended her worthy
sons."

" And he is away to the revel without good
Master Snelling's consent! Well, well, I hope
no harm will come of it. The Sheriff with his
posse may come upon them, and then—"

" The Sheriff is the worthy Thomas Luttrell
of Dunster Castle, and he is away (doubtless on
purpose; for he loves not to interfere with the

people's pastimes) in his cutter for Cleveden to bring thence his fair ward. I saw him past Blue-anchor bay, and Watchet, and nearly off Brent-knoll, as I crossed from Cardiff yester-e'en."

"Well, well; I hope no harm may come on't: nay, if I could entrust my duties to another, I would take an oar in thy row-boat, and join in the revel myself. I could wrestle once Master Jenkins; ay, you may smile, but I could indeed, though not quite so well as this young springald, Hugh de Mohun, who, they say, dorsed big Alloway, the butcher three times fairly."

"I saw him do it man, and the butcher goes with me to-day, to strive to win back his laurels; but come, we are wasting the time in talking, instead of tasting Master Richard's cheer."

The harbour-master and the captain left the pier, and entered the little inn called the Ship-aground, where we must leave them for the present, and follow the Blossom of Minehead to see what befell its crew.

CHAPTER II.

GILES Tudball, who owned and commanded the small lugger, called the Blossom of Minehead, was a short, thick-set man, posssesed of great bodily strength and mental courage. He was about thirty years of age, very healthy and active. He bore the character of a quiet, inoffensive man, and by some who knew him only on shore was deemed somewhat indolent and fond of ease, and was thought to prefer a seat in the alehouse, over a pipe and some strong waters, to attending to his business as a fellmonger. Giles had inherited this business from his father, and had, from his love of the sea and with a view of adding to his gains, joined to it the profession of a fisherman, and a carrier of goods to the opposite coast of Wales, whither he conveyed some of the cloths manufactured at Dunster, and brought back skins and hides for his own use, and woollen yarns for the use of the clothiers.

Master Jenkins's insinuations of his being engaged now and then in the contraband trade were well grounded, as Giles often ran down Channel, and returned with a great take of herrings and other fish; these, with the nets in which they were captured, concealed sundry tubs of spirits and packages of tobacco and pipes, that were considered as great luxuries in those days, and were too expensive to be procured by the lower order of the regular traders. Even the gentry were known to encourage smuggling, and to prefer the spirits and tobaccoes which had not paid duty to those which added to the revenue of the kingdom.

The contraband trade was carried on without much difficulty or danger in so insignificant a place as Minehead. There was but one revenue-officer appointed to protect the port, and he was satisfied to be on good set terms with his neighbours, and to be contented with the trifling cargoes which he was now and then permitted to seize, to make his superiors believe he was performing his duties strictly. He never wanted pipes, tobacco, or strong waters for his own use, though he never purchased them at Master Will Bowering's shop, in which his wife carried on the trade of a general dealer, while her husband went out to sea, with or without his employer, Giles Tudball. Mrs. Bowering was not offended at not having the custom-house-officer as a customer; because she thought that, in his visits to her stores, he might fancy that her goods were not purchased of the Bristol merchants, who could not afford to supply her so cheaply as her own good-man could do. Thus all parties were satisfied with the gauger, and the gauger was satisfied with all parties.

Giles Tudball moreover, kept three or four pack-horses, for the ostensible purpose of collecting and carrying home raw skins and hides, but they were frequently used for transporting inland the commodities brought up Channel in his lugger, and conveying parcels and letters for the tradesmen and gentry to their customers and friends, with whom they would otherwise have found it difficult to communicate. On these expeditions, Giles was frequently absent, as he liked a roving life, and had perfect confidence in his active and enterprising wife, Dame Tudball, as she was called, who presided over the fellmongering business, and in his mate Will Bowering, who had too good a share in the profits of the lugger, to allow him to let her remain idle in harbour.

Will Bowering was, in personal appearance, somewhat like his employer, short and strong; but he was of a talkative and rather quarrelsome disposition, especially when the marvellous tales he told over his glass, of what he saw in his trips across and down Channel, did not meet with the ready credence he demanded for them. Had the gauger been an active officer, or the people on the quay at Minehead zealously disposed towards the government, all the secrets of the smuggling transactions of the Blossom might easily have been betrayed, as Master Will, when under the influence of the strong waters of his own importation, could not keep a secret for the life of him.

With these two men in the lugger, on the morning of May-day 1642, sailed, as we have seen, a young man about seventeen or eighteen years of age; and, as he will take a prominent part in the events which I am about to relate, it will be necessary to describe his person and character, and to give a brief sketch of the little that was known of his past history.

Hugh de Mohun was slight, tall, and well-proportioned, though somewhat longer in the arms than perfect symmetry required. His face was handsome, but had rather a foreign character about it; his eyes were very dark and fringed with long black lashes; his eyebrows were finely arched, and from above his lofty forehead a profusion of coal-black hair fell in waving masses over his ears, and nearly to his shoulders; on his upper lip he wore a slight moustache, and his chin was beginning to be covered with a dark beard. His complexion was darker than an Englishman's generally is, though a ruddy glow appeared on his cheeks through the olive-coloured skin, and saved his complexion from being termed swarthy; had he been of the other sex, he would have been termed a

He was dressed like his companions, in the costume of a common sailor, which consisted of a close-
fitting vest of coarse blue Flushing cloth ; a large petticoat of the same, over loose breeches, which were
buttoned at the knees, and below them a pair of
stout, coarsely-made, water-tight boots ; round his
waist was a broad leathern girdle, in which he
carried a small pair of silver-mounted pistols, and on
his head he wore a red woollen cap, which kept back
his luxuriant hair from his forehead, and fell about
an inch below his right ear, where it terminated in a
tassel ; round his neck was suspended a small silver
chain, to which was attached a small pipe of the
same metal, and a sort of bodkin to clear the tube
of any obstruction, and to press in the tobacco, for
which purpose one end of it was flattened. Tobacco-
smoking was fashionable in those days, and every
man who had any pretensions to the rank of a gentleman carried with him his pipe and his silver to-
bacco-box as regularly as a dandy of the present
day carries his gold watch and its appurtenances.

Such, in personal appearance and dress, was the
young Hugh de Mohun, on the morning in ques-

tion: of his history all he himself knew was that he was born in London; that his father died while he was yet very young, and that his mother had retired into a religious house in Holland, to hide her grief for the loss of her husband, leaving her son to the care of Master Robert Snelling, who had been recently appointed to the incumbency of Dunster, in the room of Master Robert Browne; the said Master Robert Browne having been removed for preaching unorthodox doctrines. Master Snelling, doubtless, could have told Hugh de Mohun more of his history, had he chosen to do so; but he had not volunteered to do it, and Hugh had not as yet been very particular in his inquiries. With this infor mation, therefore, scanty as it is, the reader must be satisfied for the present.

Both Hugh de Mohun and Will Bowering were sleeping soundly on the half-deck, for they were weary; the former with his run from Dunster, whence he had escaped at a very early hour, without his tutor's knowledge or consent, and the latter from having been engaged nearly all the night in carrying and stowing away the canvass for the drinking-booth, and the barrels 𝑜𝑓 𝑏𝑒𝑒𝑟 and other articles which were intended for 𝑡𝑏𝑒 bodily comfort of the revellers on Culbone Gr𝑒𝑛. Giles Tud-ball stood at the tiller, smoking ca𝑙𝑚ly and steadily, only removing his pipe to shake o𝑢𝑡the ashes of it, or to press them with his tobacco-𝑠topper.

As the sun rose high in the heavens, the warmth of its beams awoke one 𝑜f the sleepers. "What ho! Giles Tudball, I must 𝑏𝑎ve slept some two hours at the least, and yet w𝑒 have Minchead still in view; I had thought to 𝑏𝑎𝑣e lost sight of Conygar Hill ere this, and to have r𝑜unded Bossing-ton Point and brought up at Porl𝑜ck-wear, where you know I wish to be put ashore 𝑡hat I may see the young Master Julian Bachell, 𝑎d bring him with me to the revel."

" Why Master Hugh, thou ha𝑠 𝑠lept but one short hour, and we have been drifti𝑛g with the tide only. The wind cometh but in sl𝑖ght puffs, and that at long intervals," said Giles Tuball.

" Thou should'st have whistled to it and would'st have done so had thy pipe allowe𝑑 thee, but at this rate we shall never reach C𝑢lbone; why

not out with the sweeps, as Master Luckes proposed?"

"Time enough, young sir; I care not to reach
before Master Richard, who
there by land; the captain of the St. David would
have borne me company, if it had not been for you,
and he would have had more patience

"Patience, indeed! I lack not patience more
than Master Jenkins, who, Welshman like, is impatient enough at times. I only wish to land at
Porlock, and, when I have set foot on shore at the
base of Ashley Combe, you may drift down to the
Cove as slowly as you please, to give fifty Richards
time to meet you at Culbone an you list. I
shall make bold to wake Master Will here, who
hath had as much rest as I have had, at any
rate."

"Nay, let him sleep, he has long day's work
before him," said Giles.

"His work, I trow, will rest chiefly with his
mouth, Master Tudball; what wit drinking, eating,
and telling lies, he will have enough to employ him,
and can do all that as he sits; so ere goes to rouse

drinking-booth, and the barrels of beer and other articles which were intended for the bodily comfort of the revellers on Culbone Green. Giles Tudball stood at the tiller, smoking calmly and steadily, only removing his pipe to shake out the ashes of it, or to press them with his tobacco-stopper.

As the sun rose high in the heavens, the warmth of its beams awoke one of the sleepers. "What ho! Giles Tudball, I must have slept some two hours at the least, and yet we have Minehead still in view; I had thought to have lost sight of Conygar Hill ere this, and to have rounded Bossington Point and brought up at Porlock-wear, where you know I wish to be put ashore, that I may see the young Master Julian Bachell, and bring him with me to the revel."

" Why Master Hugh, thou hast slept but one short hour, and we have been drifting with the tide only. The wind cometh but in slight puffs, and that at long intervals," said Giles Tudball.

" Thou should'st have whistled to it, and would'st have done so had thy pipe allowed thee, but at this rate we shall never reach Culbone; why

not out with the sweeps, as Master Luckes proposed ?"

" Time enough, young sir ; I care not to reach
Culbone Cove before Master Richard, who goes
there by land ; the captain of the St. David would
have borne me company, if it had not been for you,
and he would have had more patience."

" Patience, indeed! I lack not patience more
than Master Jenkins, who, Welshman like, is impatient enough at times. I only wish to land at
Porlock, and, when I have set foot on shore at the
base of Ashley Combe, you may drift down to the
Cove as slowly as you please, to give fifty Richards
time to meet you at Culbone, an you list. I
shall make bold to wake Master Will here, who
hath had as much rest as I have had, at any
rate."

" Nay, let him sleep, he has a long day's work
before him," said Giles.

" His work, I trow, will rest chiefly with his
mouth, Master Tudball ; what with drinking, eating,
and telling lies, he will have enough to employ him,
and can do all that as he sits ; so here goes to rouse

him. What ho! Will Bowering, rouse thee, man! The porpoises are rolling about, which thou may'st swear are so many mermen and mermaids, as thou hast often done before; wake up, man!" said Hugh de Mohun, applying his foot to the half-roused sleeper's person.

"I would have you know, young sir, that I will not put up with this rough usage," said Will, gazing savagely on his disturber, for he had not quite slept off the fumes of his last night's drinking; "I will not, by—"

"Tush man, thou art stale-drunk now, and a little exercise at the oar will work off the remainder of the Dutchman by the pores of the skin. So out with your sweep, and I will take the other, and a short half-hour shall see us round Bossington Point; thou cans't tell us some of thy veracious adventures as we pull along; they will serve us to laugh at."

"Come, rouse thee Will!" said Giles, "a little exercise will do thee no harm."

"I will obey *you*, as in duty bound, Master Giles, but I will be hanged ere I be commanded by a runaway stripling," said Will, slowly rising and lifting his sweep over the larboard bow.

" Thou wilt as assuredly be hanged as thou wilt venture to tell lies at the gallows' foot," said Hugh, smiling as he put out the starboard oar and began pulling; "your face now looks as if it were made up for a falsehood, only you have not courage enough to utter it; what would'st say?"

" I would say that, an thou wert a man and not a mere boy, I would make thy back intimate with the end of a two-inch rope, Master Hugh."

" I knew you were meditating a lie, Will; you dare not lay a finger on me, for fear I should serve you as I did yon bragging butcher, who boasted that he would toss me into the air as easily as one of his own bulls could do it, but who bit the grass ere he had firm hold of my collar and elbow; besides Will, thy good-nature, when thou art not in thy cups, is proverbial; and you would not injure me, who, as you know, am pledged to give thee thy belly-full to-day if you wish it."

" I wonder that the parson, good Master Suelling, does not keep his pupil under lock and key,

and flog him for breaking ward, and mumming in
sailor's clothes, instead of studying at home in a suit
of sober student's grey," said Will, recovering
his good humour, but wishing to annoy his perse-
cutor.

"Why, as to lock and key, Master Bowering,
he has strong locks and cunning too, and sleeps
with the keys under his pillow, but the windows
must be higher than the windows of the gateway
at Dunster Castle be, if he would keep Hugh de
Mohun within his walls, when he wishes to be elsewhere. I am too old for the other punishment
which you have suggested, and never bore it very
patiently; though a little more of it might
have done me good; and as to my sailor's dress, I
adopted it at your own suggestion, and gave thee
the jacobuses which purchased it at Bristol; does
it not become me?"

"Nay, I cannot but say that *you* become *it*, does
he not, Master Giles?" said Will, now restored
to good humour.

"That he does, Will, but I doubt good Master
Snelling will scold Dame Tudball, for being his

wardrobe-keeper and aiding his mumming," said Giles.

"Ah, ah! truly you make me laugh; Dame Tudball *aid* me in my freaks! why man the bell of Dunster church, in which Master Luttrell hath placed the large clock, sounded twice ere I could prevail on her to let me in to change my dress. How she did lecture me from her casement! ay and threaten to lecture you too, Giles, when she got you within the four curtains of your bed, for encouraging me in idleness and disobedience. I was forced to kiss her, Giles, when she did let me in, ere I could prevail—but thou art not jealous, eh?"

"Your kisses are too freely bestowed, Master Hugh, to make me angry that one of them be bestowed on Dame Tudball, who hath always been a discreet woman, excepting in one instance."

"Indeed! and when did she prove indiscreet?" inquired Hugh, amused at the notion of Dame Tudball, who was some ten years older than her spouse and ugly withal, going astray.

"Not in a matter of love, Master Hugh, she is

not amorously bent, but she showed her weak-
ness in going to Watchett-Point to see a merman,
which Will Bowering, there, assured her, with
many oaths, he himself saw combing and brushing
his sea-green locks."

"Not so, not so ; I do swear by St. Philip and
St. James, it was not so : that I saw the merman,
I am ready to testify before the Parliament ; but
Dame Tudball rode the skewball mare to Watch-
ett, to see the tobacco-pipe of old Master Luckes the
harbour-master of Minyead, which was found in
the belly of a porpoise with other curiosities," said
Will.

"And what were they?" said Hugh, laughing
aside at the captain.

"I cannot recollect them all just now, my master, but I know that a pewter measure and a shirt
of guernsey-work belonging to young Master Richard Luckes were among the number; and the pipe
I saw with my own eyes."

"Why thou art growing worse than ever, Will!"
said his master, "I have heard you tell these lies
at night after your allowance of strong waters, but

never in your sober moments; you know that the harbour-master's pipe was picked up by the tailor, as he groped for congers, in Blue-anchor bay, and that the Guernsey frock and the pewter measure were borrowed by yourself, when you went in Master Jenkins's cutter after alabaster from Watchett cliff for the masons. Master Jenkins says that his metheglin made you so uproarious, that you threw off the shirt to fight his mate, and tossed the pewter measure at his head, when he tried to prevent you making an ass of yourself."

"Well! well! be it so. I am not used to his honey-wine, and it might have overpowered me; but as to the merman, I will swear to having seen him with my own eyes, as plainly as I now see the Blue-anchor hostel at Porlock-wear," said Will.

"Was it before noon or after?" inquired Hugh de Mohun, looking as seriously as he could.

"It was at night, Master Hugh, the moon was shining as I lay at anchor in this very craft, with my lines out stem and starn, fishing for cod, or tublings, or any thing that might come to hook."

"And you saw the merman distinctly?"

" Why, he came alongside, and looked so wist-
fully in my face, that I was about to offer him a
drink of my liquor, when he turned down and
splashed me with his tail as he dived below."

Giles Tudball and the young man here burst
into a loud roar of laughter, which so offended
Will, that he turned sulky and said no more until
they reached the landing-place at Porlock-wear,
where they put Master Hugh ashore.

CHAPTER III.

As soon as Hugh de Mohun had left the boat which put him ashore at Porlock-wear, he walked up to the little inn called the Blue Anchor, where he meditated breaking his fast.

When he entered the kitchen, he found a table spread out with cold meats and pies, salted and dried fish, and abundance of ale and cider. The host himself was presiding at the feast, which was partaken of by a motley crew, who were evidently on their way to the revel. At one end sat a group of gipsies by themselves, talking in a language peculiar to that extraordinary race of people; by their sides lay bundles of sticks, and bags containing tin boxes and other painted toys, which were, even in those days, set up to be

thrown at by the visitors at junketings and revels : at another part of the table sat a company
of minstrels, having their rebecs, pipes and tabors,
and other instruments for rustic music, within
a convenient distance of them : a band of morris-dancers, with their little bells affixed to their
knees and their wrists, sat next ; and, at the head
of the table, in colloquy with the host, was seated
a mediciner or quack-doctor, with his man, the
Merry Andrew as he is called.

Beneath the bench on which they sat, was placed
the box in which the doctor carried his panaceas,
and on it rested the large tin horn, with which
his servant summoned all who had ailments of
of any kind to come and purchase a certain cure
for them.   Some half-dozen stout, sturdy men,
clad in close-fitting cloth dresses, and having thick,
heavy-nailed boots on their feet, and padded stock-
ings on their legs, stood together in another part
of the room, and were evidently come from the
hills, to try a fall in wrestling with any one who
should be bold enough to oppose them.

They eyed the youthful Hugh de Mohun as

he entered the hostelry, and a whisper passed among them that he was the stripling who had given the bullying butcher of Minyead three fair falls, a fact which seemed to excite their wonder and their smiles.

Hugh, however, noticed them not, but, going up to the head of the table, after saluting the host and Doctor Graveboys, he seized a huge round of corned beef, helped himself liberally from the joint, and washed down the mass of solids with huge draughts from a black jack of foaming ale; after which he picked the bones of a salted herring or two, and finished his meal with some eggs, which were placed in a basin before him.

"I'faith, master mine," said the doctor's servant, in a subdued tone, but loud enough to be heard by the host and his young guest; "if all be true that you say of your wondrous powders for procuring an appetite, the young seaman there must have been a good customer and bought largely."

"His appetite, Jansen, is the result of health and exercise, and probably of a prolonged fast, which has caused the juices of the stomach to irri-

throv
vels :
of mii.
and otl
a convei
ris-danc
knees an
of the tal
a medicin
Merry Ar
   Beneath
the box in
and on itr
his servai
of a'
       So.
    cke-fitti

10 men

ve not

ipling,

ishmen

ıfairly,

vering,

Ship-

should

i com-

anage

well;

eace,

g in

de-

the

ent

tate the *fauces.* My powders, of which you speak, are intended only for such as, having indulged in over-much eating and especially in the use of strong waters, which are poison to indolent sit-at-homes, have not energy enough to seek a renewal of their digestive powers by the free use of their limbs in the free air of heaven."

"You say right, Master Graveboys," said the host, "strong waters ought never to be resorted to but by such as have taken a chill, or would qualify themselves for exposure to the severity of the weather, or the dews of the late night or early morning."

"And for which of these dost thou apply so frequently to the little squab bottle of true Dutch build, which stands in yonder buffet, worthy host?" asked Hugh de Mohun, as he pushed the emptied jack from before him.

"I am troubled with the wind-colic at times, Master Hugh, and though I try a little ginger in my ale, it will not always remove it without some little qualification," said the host.

"Jansen," cried the doctor, "open the chest and

give me a small bottle of my elixir of life; our host shall pay himself for our meal therewith, and find much ease in his ailments without resorting to the Dutchman."

"Nay, nay, sit still man. I would rather take thy master's coins than his cordials at any time, and this morning my ale sits sufficiently easy on my stomach," said the host.

"Well, well, Jansen," said the doctor, a little disconcerted at seeing Hugh smile, "find, if thou canst, a box of my pills for refreshing the brain which has been strained by over-much study: the student of Dunster there, may perhaps like to purchase and try them when he puts off his mumming dress and applies himself to his humanities again."

"Spare yourself the trouble, man; but, if your chest possesses a philtre or love-potion, give it to the doctor that he may prevail for a kiss with the fair tapstress of the Luttrel Arms in Dunster, from whom he hath hitherto extorted nothing but sound and well-deserved boxes on the ear."

"Or rather, bring out the salve which has sovereign virtues in allaying the pains and aches which

result from heavy falls; for the butcher will doubtless be at Culbone to redeem his lost honour as a
wrestler."

"Keep thy salve for thyself, doctor, if it be
good for a broken head; for I think it not impossible that your impertinent tongue may earn you
a cracked crown ere the day be past," said Hugh
smiling good-naturedly.

"Not from you, young sir, you are too much of
a man to lay hands upon the old' and peaceable, and I trust, if the butcher of Minyead comes
to try a fall, you will serve him as you did before, and as he richly deserves to be served, who
bullies and crows over those whose strength is
not a match for his."

"I would gladly see him grassed," said Jansen,
"for he is a braggart, and abuseth his bulky
strength."

"And so you shall, Jansen, if my eye and foot
fail me not, and he provokes me to the contest.
I have no quarrel with the man, but I shall not
decline a fall with him if he seek it," said Hugh.

"It were well," whispered the host, "you had

your friends by you to see fair play. The men from the hills will be there, and they love not to see one of their company foiled by a stripling, and he of gentle blood."

"Tush, man, never fear for me; Englishmen will see fair play, and if for once they act unfairly, know that Giles Tudball and Will Bowering, with Master Jenkins and the host of the Ship-aground, will be there to stand by me, even should young Julian Bachell refuse to give me his company to the Green."

"He will not refuse you, sir, if he can manage to get away with you, he loves sport too well; but his father, who is a justice of the peace, would not that his son should be seen aiding in games which Pym and the Parliament have declared unlawful."

"The crop-eared knaves will not induce the owner of Ashley Combe to interfere and prevent our innocent games," said Hugh.

"I said not that he would interfere," said the host; "but he would rather that his son should not join in them."

"Well, having paid my reckoning, and thank-
ed you for your hospitality and good cheer, and the
mediciner there for his offer of pills and ointments,
I will away to Master Julian and learn his inten-
tions," said Hugh, throwing the price of his break-
fast on the table, and preparing to leave the room.

"Should occasion call for them, command my
services, young sir, and those of my servant Jansen," said the doctor with a meaning look.

Hugh smiled as he bade adieu to him, and, passing through the back of the house, sprung up
the steep ascent which led through the garden of
the inn to the road from Porlock to Ashley Combe.

The Lodge in which Master Bachell, the Lord
of the Manor, dwelt, was perched, as it were, in a
small recess in the mighty cliffs which overhang
the Channel above Porlock-wear. The ascent to it
was very steep, and it was in those days only
accessible to horsemen and persons on foot. The
road was very narrow, and composed of loose, large
stones, the *débris* of the red sand-stone rocks of
which the cliff is composed. It was overhung by
the branches of the dwarf oaks and ashes, with

which the surface of these hills is clothed, and which afforded a safe and much sought shelter to the red deer with which the country abounded.

The house was built of the red rock, and from the Channel appeared to be a part of the cliff itself. It was not discernible from the road until you stood in front of it, at the gate of the lodge which admitted you into its grounds.

Up this steep and broken road Hugh de Mohun sprung as lightly and as actively as one of the red deer, the denizens of the neighbouring woods, would have done. He paused not to gaze at the splendid prospect which, at intervals, might be gained through openings in the coppices, but hurried on,- as if business and not pleasure urged him. Just as he reached the path which turned out of the main track, the bridle-road from Porlock to Culbone, he overtook Master Richard Luckes, the host of the Ship Aground on Minehead quay, who was riding on a stout galloway, with his wife seated on a pillion behind him.

Hugh exchanged salutations with them, and was about to leave them to pursue their way, when

Master Richard told him to keep his wind, and not to over-exert himself, for that he had seen Alloway, the big butcher, push off in Master Jenkins's boat, and had heard him say that the parson's runaway pupil should rue the day when he dorsed, by accident, the best wrestler below the hills.

Hugh smiled, nodded his head confidently, and told Master Richard that he was not frightened at the bully's threats. They then parted, and the young man entered the gate-lodge of Ashley Combe, and bade the gate-keeper seek Master Julian Bachell and tell him that he wished to speak with him.

" Why not walk up to the house, sir ? " said the porter; " you will find both my old master and the young squire within."

" I would speak to Master Julian alone," said Hugh, " and care not that his father should know of my being here ; you understand me ?"

" Ay—ay, I can easily believe that, Master Hugh de Mohun having doffed his student's grey, and donned a mummer's dress, would fain entice his friend, Julian Bachell, unbeknown to his father, to the revels at Culbone."

" You are not far wrong, old man, and as you are no spoil-sport, and would not betray your young master, seek him to do my errand," said Hugh, placing a piece of silver in the porter's hand to quicken his movements.

Hugh waited, and not very patiently it must be owned, for some quarter of an hour ere his messenger returned, to say that Master Julian would be with him as soon as he could leave the library without exciting his father's suspicions.

"I had great difficulty in getting your message delivered, young sir, for Master Julian was clo- seted with his father, reading to him the letters which came down from London this morning. I was forced to send in Hodge, the keeper, to say that one of the blood-hound pups was, he thought, down in the distemper. I knew that wou'd bring him out if anything would, for he loves his dogs, and would grieve sorely to lose one of his favourite breed. He readily forgave my deceiving of him, as you may believe, when he heard that the pup was well, and that you were wishing to see him · he will be here anon."

Hugh passed the time in talking to the old man about the hounds and red deer, and the woodcocks and wild-fowl that he had killed in his younger days, until Julian made his appearance. The young men shook hands heartily, and expressed their joy at seeing each other.

Julian Bachell was about a year older than Hugh de Mohun. He was nearly as tall but much stouter; and, though such was not the case, appeared to be a far more powerful man. His face was very fair, and his hair and eyes light; his countenance wore a bright and cheerful look although there was a something about the short upper lip, and the lines about the mouth, that indicated pride, and perhaps a hasty temper. He was dressed plainly in a suit of claret-coloured cloth, and wore on his head a low-crowned broad-brimmed hat, with a drooping feather in it, and had a light rapier by his side. His right hand held a small riding-wand, and on his left arm rested a beautiful small black and tanned spaniel, whose curly ears quite covered its tiny face, and hung some inch or two below its mouth.

"Why, how now!" said Master Julian, as he dropped the riding-wand to enable him to grasp
Hugh's extended hand. "What brings Master
Snelling's hopeful pupil to Ashley Combe this
morning, mummed out in a suit of Giles Tudball's
ordering, doubtless? though, faith, it becomes him
well."

"Nay, no flattery, you know I am fond of the
sea, and Will Bowering prevailed on me to let
him buy me this dress in Bristol, lest, as he said
the tar should adhere to my sober grey and betray me by its odour to the good parson, who
fondly believes that I am sleeping or studying
over the gateway of Dunster Castle, when I am
whistling for the wind in mid-channel, and taking
a midnight trip to the opposite coast."

"And you have walked over some ten miles from
Dunster just to show me how well the suit becomes you."

"Not so, Julian; I sailed, or rather pulled in
Giles Tudball's lugger from Minehead quay to
Porlock-wear this morning, and I am here, after
having done justice to mine host's beef at the Blue

Anchor below, to ask you to join me in a walk
to Culbone to see the revels."

"The revels, man! art mad? do not you know
that they are forbidden to be held, under pain of
the displeasure of the puritan Parliament?"

"I do know it; but I do not think that any
one of the Parliament will be likely to hear of
a revel being held in so retired a spot as Culbone is."

"Why, man, smell I not of parchment? I was
reading over a most stringent document, sent down
by Master Speaker to my father as a justice of the
peace, warning him to put a stop to this same
Culbone revel, when your messenger called me
from the library with his tale of a distempered
puppy."

"There must be spies about, Julian, or so con-
temptible a business as a revel at Culbone would
never have reached the Speaker's ears; but what
will Master Bachell do? he will not prevent our old
English sports and pastimes."

"My father, Julian, has business which obliges
him to ride in a contrary direction from

Culbone to-day, and he knows not, of his own knowledge, that a revel is to be held."

"Good!" said Hugh smiling, " I knew that so loyal a subject as Master Bachell would not obey the orders of a set of canting knaves, who would oppress the whole nation, and deprive them of their rights and privileges, just as they are trying to deprive their lawful sovereign of his prerogatives."

" Hugh de Mohun, you are right, and were it not that I might subject my father to inconvenience and perhaps to danger, for the Puritans love to catch a gentleman and trounce him if they can, I would even join thee in this revelling; but, as it is, I would rather dissuade you from going."

" Julian, I have pledged my word."

" Pledged your word ? to whom ? "

" You will smile, when I name Alloway, the butcher, of Minehead."

" He whom you threw so fairly three falls ? "

" The same," said Hugh, " he lays it to accident, and is gone in Master Jenkins' boat to give me the meeting on Culbone green."

" Nay then, for the honour of Dunster, you must indulge him; and. as it may be dangerus to go alone, for the wrestlers hang togethe like freemasons, I will go with you," said allan Bachell.

"For that matter, I am not badly suppted: I have Giles Tudball and his mate, Master Jenkins, and the host of the Ship-aground of Lnc-head quay: moreover I have promise of aid rom the strange old mediciner—"

"Mean you Graveboys, who writes hinself M. D. though he hath not a diploma even in the northern colleges ?"

" Even so; and his man Jansen."

" Then trust me you might have worse allie for the doctor is doubtless a descendant of Dr. Faustus, and knows more, though not *in artene-dendi*, than people give him credit for; but I ill put on a mumming dress to join thee."

"Not to the injury of your father," said Huh.

" I will so alter my personal appearance, hat not even he who begat me should know me."

Thus saying, Julian left the gate-house, nd

returned in about ten minutes dressed in the livery of one of the keepers of Exmoor forest ; by the aid of a wig and corked eyebrows, moustache, an imperial, and a large broad-flapped deer-skin cap, the disguise seemed to Hugh to be perfect.

CHAPTER IV.

THE little village of Culbone lies about two short miles from Ashley Combe Lodge. The road to it is made through the thick plantations of stunted oak and dwarf ash, which cover the lofty hills rising immediately above the Channel. It is very narrow and steep, and passable only by horsemen or persons on foot, and requires a firm step and keen eye to enable horse or man to keep on his legs ; for the large unshapely fragments of rock, of which it is fashioned, are loosened and rolled down in wild disorder by the heavy storms, which are attracted by the woods and lofty mountains skirting this side of the Bristol Channel.

Hugh de Mohun and Julian Bachell climbed

the first ascent in silence, for there was not room for them to walk abreast, and it was no easy matter to find breath for discourse, when the lungs were in full play, from the exertion required in mastering the difficulties of a path, which was nearly as steep as the roof of a house, and formed of loose and slippery materials.

When they gained the top of the first steep, they paused to take breath, and to view the extensive and interesting prospect, which an opening in the woods through a deep combe afforded them.

Immediately in front of them was the mouth of the Bristol Channel, with its bold, majestic foreland, behind which lay Linton and Ly'mouth, and opposite to which in mid-channel is Lundy Island. To the right lay the coast of South Wales, studded with towns and churches, and having for its background a long and high ridge of mountains; still more to the right and almost behind the gazers, lay the bold headland called Bossington-Point, and in the bay which it forms lay snugly ensconced the little town of Porlock, with its quaint church-steeple, and about a mile nearer to them

the hamlet of Porlock-wear which boasts of one
public and three private houses occupied by fisher-
men, whose boats might be seen lying in a little
basin, which is filled at high tides, and is called
the wear.   Immediately below their feet, on the
side of the steep hill which they had climbed, was
Ashley Combe Lodge, amid a mass of wood which
fringed the very borders of the Channel.

It was as brilliant a May-day as ever shone
from the heavens, and, as the coast of Somersetshire
is warm and genial, and favourable to vegetation—
for there the myrtle and other tender plants flou-
rish through the winter—the trees had put on their
new livery of brightest green, and the birds, with
which the woods were filled, cheered their mates
as they brooded on their eggs with every variety
of song, in which the nightingale's note was pre-
dominant.   A few fleecy clouds floated beneath
the blue sky, and seemed to be reflections of the
white canvass sails of the vessels, which dotted
here and there the surface of the sparkling
sea.

"On my word Master Hugh," said Julian, after

a prolonged silence, and with brightening eye, "it were worth more than a pair of exhausted lungs and strained knees to gain such a glorious sight as this. North Devon may boast of its rocks, and caverns, and iron-bound coast, but give me my much-loved Somersetshire, with its well-clad mountains' and leafy combes, down which the brook dashes and splashes, in haste to contribute its support to the fulness of our glorious Channel. Even our very Tors, covered only with scanty heath, the brown fern, and the yellow furze, have charms for me. With my dog and my fowling gun, and my horses and trusty deer-hounds, I could live here all my days without a sigh, and leave the troubles and turmoils of towns and cities to those who love them."

"It is a glorious sight, this coast, Julian," replied his companion, "especially when beheld from the sea and by the light of a brilliant moon: I have spent hours in gazing upon it, yet, I have often thought that I would rather steer some goodly bark out into broad ocean yonder, and visit other lands, in search of fame and wild adventures, than settle calmly down as a country gentleman, whose only excitement is the chase—even in so lovely a spot as this. I would herd with men who war with their fellows, and not with beasts and birds, Julian, and I would e'en consent to dwell in some crowded city, provided I might mingle with the great and the brave, and share their councils and emulate their deeds."

" Nay, speak not contemptuously of the chase, which our greatest and our bravest love because it is a mimic warfare, and calls for plots and stratagems, deep designs, and boldly executed deeds, to ensure success in it. It is no place for the coward, Hugh ; the slinking hound, the low-bred, timid horse, and the fearful rider, are best away from it. Give me a noble steed and my stanch hounds; let me hear their cheerful notes mingling with the joyous blasts of the horn, as we fly over our hills and dales, and dash through woods and over brooks in our course, until, when horses, hounds, and men are nearly exhausted from exertion and excitement, the quarry is in view, and we rush gloriously in and kill—"

" A timid deer !'" said Hugh, looking down upon

the ground, as if he saw the panting beast before him, and grieved, like the melancholy Jacques, for the death of so noble an animal.

"A timid deer! no man, a mighty stag, with antlered head, who stands at bay and—"

"Gores the noble hounds, until some hunter, bolder than the rest, hamstrings the beast, and all around enjoy the sight of the tears trickling from its lustrous eyes, as the dogs tear it to the ground. A rush of the huntsmen and a knife drawn across its dappled throat and all is over."

"Not so, Master Hugh," said Julian dropping his excited tone and smiling, "what think you of the noble haunch, the savoury pasty and the tale of dangers encountered and overcome, recited over the purple wine-cup?"

"I think that some, but not such as you, Julian love that part of the chase best. You know I am never backward to join your hunt, and am no laggard in the pursuit; but I would fly at higher game: were I a hawk or a falcon now, I would seek my native rocks and woods, and quit a master who would fly me at the timid partridge or sluggish

wild-duck when my proper quarry is the courageous heron with its spear-like bill, upon which I
would rather be impaled than let my noble nature
be debased.   But let us on; see yonder, in the shel
tered cove of Culbone lies the crewless lugger of
Giles Tudball; and, as I live, below us, gliding
stealthily beneath the trees that fringe the shore, is
the boat of Master Jenkins, which bears mine adversary to the fray.   So, on Julian, we must be there
to give them the meeting, and a race up these
steeps will give me a breathing, that will prepare
my lungs and limbs for the struggle."

Thus saying, Hugh de Mohun led the way up
the tortuous path, at a speed which prevented any
further converse, until they reached the summit of
the hill and saw below them the miniature church
of Culbone and its three little white cottages on
the Green, which was studded here and there with
groups of people and canvass tents and booths.

A few minutes brought them down the rapid
descent to the brook, which boiled and fumed
as it struggled over its stony bed from the hill above,
and hastened to close its short career in the sea,

which indented the coast below with its salt
waves, as if eager to meet and welcome the fine,
fresh draught supplied by the Dryades of the Porlock hills from their caves and retreats. Before they
crossed the brook, by means of the large fragments
of rock, which were placed at certain intervals in its
bed to insure dry feet to pedestrians, Julian begged
his friend to consider that he wished not to be
known, and, for the better concealment of his real
character, should prefer quitting his side, unless any
particular occurrence should render it necessary for
him to join him, and that he would then do so as a
serving-man and not as an equal.

Hugh, who was anxious to prevent any unpleasant consequences resulting to his friend from his
compliance with his whims, readily yielded his consent, and, leaving him behind, crossed the brook,
and quickly ensconced himself in the booth erected
by Master Luckes for the entertainment of his customers. Hugh found Giles Tudball and Master
Will Bowering, seated within, on a plank which
rested on two barrels into which spigots had been inserted, ready for those whose exertions should cause

them to need either stimulants or refreshments.
Master Tudball was quietly smoking his intermina-
ble pipe, and his mate was following so laudable an
example, only removing it now and then, to tell some
miraculous tale to Mistress Luckes, who presided
at a sort of temporary counter, whence she supplied
strong waters to those who prefered them to ale and
cider. A table, formed of the bretting or bottom
boards of the lugger, was covered with a good store
of solid food, and was put under the care and su-
perintendence of Master Jenkins, who acted as
carver, to relieve the host, whose duties were confined to the ale-can and the cider-cup.

Master Richard, the host, was the first to sa-
lute Hugh de Mohun, and to ask him if he would
eat of what was set out, or drink a draught from
his barrels, to quench his thirst after his walk over
the bill. This he declined, but, the hostess pressing
him to become her customer, he took a small quantity of spirit and mixed it in a cup with some
water, and then seated himself by Giles Tudball, and
filled and lighted his pipe. There were no strangers in the booth, for the company had not yet

arrived in great numbers, and the few that had arrived were employed in tethering and foddering the sumpter horses and forest ponies, on which they had travelled, in the wood adjoining. Hugh, knowing that he could trust his hearers with the secret without fear of its betrayal, told them briefly that Master Julian Bachell had accompanied him to the revel, disguised as a forester, and did not wish to be known, lest it might involve his father in difficulties, as he had had notice from Master Pym and the Parliament to prevent the revels taking place. All agreed, therefore, not to appear to know him when he came amongst them during the festivities of the day.

"But where," asked Hugh of the captain of the St. David, "is my redoubtable foe, the burly butcher of Minyead?"

"He is above there, master mine, in the tent of the hill-wrestlers, arranging the play for the day, and is not in the best of humours, from having been teased and bantered on his former defeat, by Master Richard's father, the harbour-master, before we left the quay; thou must be alive,

young sir, or he will make thy bones sore if he
catches thee at a disadvantage."

Hugh only smiled in reply to this advice, and
sat smoking his pipe, and conversing at intervals
in a whisper with Giles Tudball, and laughing
at the lies told to the incredulous hostess by
the mate of the lugger.

Julian Bachell, in the mean while crossed the
brook, and strolled towards the groups on the green ;
there he found the gipsies preparing for the
amusement of their expected customers, by making circular holes in the ground and driving their
stakes into the centre of them. The minstrels
had formed a sort of temporary theatre under a
large oak, by suspending coloured canvass hangings from the lower branches, having taken care
to secure a smooth surface within a few yards of
them, whereon the lads and lasses, who were so
disposed, might figure in the mazy dance to the
sound of their music. Beyond them again were
the morris-dancers, seated round a pannier, which
contained the handkerchiefs, sticks, and the fool's
baton and bladder, and other auxiliaries of their

simple art. The wrestlers were, as Master Jenkins had said, in a tent by themselves, arranging
the sports of the day, in which they were to take
a prominent part.

Julian looked in upon them as he passed by,
but was bidden by Master Alloway to " look after
his own concerns and not to trouble himself with
what did not belong to him." At any other time
the butcher would have been greeted on the
head with a blow of the stout ashen beating-pole,
which the seeming forester carried in his hand, in
return for his insolence; but he was suffered to go
unpunished for reasons which may be easily divined.

Julian turned away towards the platform, which
was a sort of turf mound, raised about three feet
above the level ground, in order that all the spectators might see the wrestling and the back-sword
playing to advantage. In the centre of the
green was erected the May-pole, of tall, smooth,
polished wood, tapering away to a fine point, to
which was suspended by gay-colored ribbons a
huge leg of mutton; he who could reach it and
take it down was to have it for his pains. At its

foot were placed some half dozen sacks, in which a race was to be run round the green, and a large hand-bell for the sport called jingling.

Without the green, and under the shadow of a large tree, was a small table, converted into a stage, on which Dr. Graveboys had taken his station, ready to sell his nostrums when his easily-deluded customers should arrive ; and by his side stood Master Jansen, trumpet in hand, with the box of medicines suspended in front of him by a broad strap which passed over his shoulders.

The doctor, as Julian passed, looked earnestly at him, and then, throwing his eyes round him to see that his movements were not observed, made a slight bow of recognition, which the young man did not acknowledge, but passed on under the shade of the trees, where the horses of those who had reached Culbone were tethered, to a retired spot, where he threw himself on the ground to watch the proceedings of the rustics, who where now beginning to assemble from all quarters, but more especially from the road by which he had himself travelled, and from another formed along the side of the brook which descended from the hill above.

Among these, especially the latter, who had evidently gone by a round-about way to avoid notice, he observed many of his father's tenants, farm-servants, and forest-keepers. Those, who came by the more frequented track, principally consisted of tradesmen and fishermen from Mine-head, Alcombe, Dunster, and Porlock. To see if his disguise were perfect, Julian boldly sauntered among the people from Ashley Combe and Porlock.

Although they stared hard at him as he passed, he was convinced that he was unknown and unsus-pected by all but one, and that a young girl, the daughter of the gate-keeper, who had doubtless been apprised of his going by her father, and bid-den not to betray his secret or to notice him. She accordingly dropped her eyes when she saw him gaze at her, and betrayed only by a blush her recognition of her young master.

Satisfied with the result of this experiment, Julian left his lurking-place under the trees, and boldly crossed the green, which was now more thickly

studded with merry faces and stalwart limbs
than when he crossed it before, and entered the
booth of Master Richard Luckes. No notice was
taken of his entrance by any one, and, after he had
accepted an offer of a pipe and some cider from the
host, who treated him as a common customer, he
seated himself near to Hugh de Mohun and Giles
Tudball.

He had not been long seated ere Master Jansen
entered the booth, and, passing by the host, declined his offer of " Drink friend, drink! barley-
juice or the real golden-pippin cider," walked
straight up to the hostess and, assuring her that
he was ill and that the doctor's nostrums were
not to his taste, for he knew their component parts,
begged to be indulged with a glass of her Dutch
fire-water.

While she turned her back to him to supply
his wants, he slipped a piece of paper into Julian's
hand, and, having drunk and paid for his cordial,
vanished, assuring the company that "his plan
had been succesful, and that he felt very much re-
lieved."

Julian cautiously opened and read the paper thus cautiously given to him. Its contents were these—" I have just heard that the revel will be interrupted ; but do all you can, with your friends, to induce the people to disperse quietly : above all things, do not *you* be seen or known ; and it were well that G. T. have his lugger ready to convey H. D. M. off at a moment's notice."

A. G.

Julian, who did not doubt that Aaron Graveboys wrote the scroll, shewed it to Hugh and to Giles, who, although they could not comprehend the meaning of the writer, resolved to prepare to obey his orders.

CHAPTER V.

WE must enter the tent erected for the wrestlers, and see what is going on within its canvass
walls.

Alloway, whose name has been so often mentioned as the burly butcher who had been fairly
thrown three times by Hugh de Mohun, was sitting on the ground apart from the rest. He had
been laughed at and taunted by so many about
his defeat, that he was in a very bad humour, nor
could the pipe and stout ale, with which he was
endeavouring to console himself and to strengthen
his nerves for the anticipated play, dispel the
malignant feelings which he entertained towards his youthful adversary. He felt very spite-

ful towards everybody, and resolved to concen-
trate his venom and spit it out on him who was
the cause of all his vexations.

" Well butcher," said one of the wrestlers, turning from his companions towards Alloway, "as
the struggle between you and the stripling will
be severe, we have agreed that you shall not waste
your strength by joining in the general play, but
reserve yourself for a single bout which, as the most
interesting, shall come off last."

" By knife and cleaver, I swear, I will not be
thwarted thus," said Alloway. "I came here to
take my part in the trials of strength, and I will
not be put off. The man who can fell an ox, even
one of the large Devon breed, by a single blow
of his arm, and carry the carcass, at twice, upon his
shoulders from the slaughter-house to the market
shambles, is not to be cheated of his honours in the
ring, because he has to try a fall with a mere
youth—"

" Who hath had the best in three fair bouts,"
said the wrestler.

" By accident—by accident—I swear by knife

and cleaver—a good butcher's oath—it was by mere accident."

"Ay, accidents will happen, is an old saying, and they may happen again, Master Alloway, so reserve thyself for the struggle on which will depend the honour of the wrestlers of Minyead. If thou art defeated, thy townsmen will not be thought worthy to meet the hill-men on fair terms; we must *give* thee a fall or two to put you on an equality with us in future, as the swift runner gives his slower adversary a few yards in the start."

"Fear not for me, I will throw the herring-gutted boy, or I will die in the ring ; but I will not be put aside like a weak bow, which is only stretched the moment the arrow is to be placed on the string, for fear it should lose its spring. I will try a fall in my turn, by G—d!"

"It cannot be; we have arranged the play without you, three against three; but if you throw the stripling, and your mind be then unchanged, you shall take up the conqueror, and so win the prize from all of us, if you can."

To this proposition, Alloway, after holding out a long time, at last consented. He left the tent, with his pipe in his mouth and his black jack of ale in his hand, and was followed by the others to the platform, where the single-stick players had already taken their station, to commence the sports of the day

Master Richard Luckes, who presided over the play, called the combatants by name, beginning with the less skilful, who quickly drew blood from each others' crowns, amid the shouts of the bystanders, and gave place to others more skilful in the use of the basket-stick.

After an hour's play, which was pronounced most excellent by the best judges, the platform was left in possession of an old man, who had had one of his eyes knocked out, in a severe struggle which he continued after he had removed the eye and found that "there was no *blood*."

This man was the champion of the country round, and no one cared to oppose him, so that he was putting on his upper coat, preparing to leave the platform and claim the prize, when Master Richard Luckes bade him wait while he summoned the company three times, to see if none could be found to try another bout with him.

To the first summons, uttered in a clear loud voice no one responded.

"It is of no use," said one of the beaten players wiping the blood from his forehead," his weapon flies quicker than the eye can follow it, and before you can stop it—crack! your eyes flash lightning and your crown is broken."

"You may as well strike at a will o'the wisp," said another. " He was here before you, and when the blow descends, hey presto! he is there behind you—the devil aids him I think."

" Devil me no devil," said Giles Tudball; "if I did not despise the childish play, I would try a bout with him myself for the honour of Minyead. Can no one be found to risk a cracked crown ?"

A dead silence followed, and the old man chuckled and looked round triumphantly.

The summons was uttered for the second time

but produced nothing but a low murmur from the spectators.

"For the third and last time," said Richard Luckes, "I pronounce the stage in possession of old Master Castle, the sheep-drover of Berkshire, and the prize to be his, if no one will come forward for the honour of Somerset."

"Stand aside there," called out Will Bowering. "Make way, make way," shouted the crowd, closing together instead of falling back, that they might get a sight of the individual who was rash enough to try conclusions with the veteran. Aided by Giles Tudball and some dozen more, two young men, the one dressed as a forest-keeper and the other as a sailor, forced their way through the crowd to the side of the turf-stage. The former took his station at the side, and the latter sprang lightly upon the platform and took a basket stick from Master Richard Luckes.

"It is the student of Dunster," shouted those who knew Hugh de Mohun.

"Ay, and if Master parson Snelling have driven learning into his head, the Berkshire sheep-drover will not be long in making a hole whence it may ooze out again with his hot blood," said Master Alloway.

" And all the better for you, butcher," said one of the wrestlers, " he will be the better qualified to try a fall with you, when his strength is a little reduced."

" In the name of Heaven," said the fair hostess, Mistress Luckes, "the young wildgoose is not going to risk his handsome head in a struggle with a man who has cracked as many human crowns as he has paid crowns of silver for Porlock sheep!"

" That will he," replied Master Jenkins, " he hath but little regard for life or limb when honour is at stake."

" Then I will e'en seek Master Graveboys and bid him spread a plaister, while I prepare my scissors to cut off some of those flowing locks, from which he has withdrawn his woollen cap to make his fate the surer," said Mrs. Luckes.

As she said, Hugh de Mohun, after selecting a weapon, and shaking the hand of his adversary to prove that no malice existed between them, threw off his cap according to the rules of the game. His long dark hair, which had been partially confined by it, fell down over his ears and nearly rested on his shoulders.

" Keep a ready hand, a quick eye, and an active foot, Hugh, or the old man will be too much for you," said Giles Tudball.

Hugh smiled and took his ground. His right foot was slightly advanced, and his stick held in such a manner as to be ready to protect his head or to assail his adversary.

A long pause took place, amidst a breathless silence; both stood on the defensive and seemed unwilling to give the first blow: at length, Hugh dropped his stick a little, and, quick as lightning, the old man, seeing what he thought an opening, struck at his head. Hugh sprung back, the turf received the blow, and, before the old man could recover his guard, Hugh, instead of striking St. George, as the blow at the head is termed, gave point as if his stick had been a rapier. The old man staggered and fell on his back. Master Richard stooped over him, and found that his scalp had been abraded

for about three inches, and that the blood was running from the wound in a decided stream.

A loud shout rent the air, when the fact was
made known, and, amidst reiterated cries of "Somerset for ever!" Hugh was declared the victor. The
three challenges were again given out but no one
replied to them. The prize, a new hat of the
sort worn by countrymen, was given to the victor,
who insisted on Master Castle wearing it for his
sake, and to hide the ugly wound on his hitherto
invincible head.

The old man accepted the hat, saying that he
had been fairly beaten, but by a trick that he had
never seen practised before.

" Thanks to my fencing-master," said Hugh, as
he jumped from the stage, "I have achieved a very
easy victory."

" Make way there, make way for Doctor Graveboys," screamed Mistress Luckes, "he hath a sovereign remedy for broken pates."

" Permit me to apply this never-failing *unguen-
tum* to your wounded head," said the doctor, ad-
dressing old Master Castle.

" I will see thee and thy Ann Quintin at the devil first; a little cold water will soon stanch the blood, aided by a few pinches of beaver from my hat; and a quart or two of strong ale will allay the pain."

" And produce inflammation," said the doctor. " Jansen bring a bottle of my *elixir vitæ*."

" He licks her what ? " said the old man, giving Jansen such a thrust with his elbow as nearly up-set him and his box of medicaments. " I tell thee I will ha' none of thy filthy drugs, but will hasten to the booth of Master Luckes, and confer a cup of good ale on yonder lad, who is gamesome and ge-nerons both."

Hugh declined the offer, and left his antagonist to go with Giles Tudball to see the climbing for the leg of mutton, a prize that Master Will Bower-ing carried off, after he had permitted several coun-try competitors to rub all the grease off the pole in their attempts to reach it.

Next followed a race after a huge pig, with a very short and well-soaped tail. This afforded most excellent sport, as the animal, being used to his native woods, in which he gained his autumnal pursuers a dance that they did not forget for many a day. After being chased for nearly an hour, he fairly gave them the slip, and they returned to the green with torn clothes and wounded limbs, to be laughed at by their friends.

Then came on the jingling-match, which is thus played. Six men toss up which of them shall first bear the bell; he upon whom the lot falls strips to the waist, and fastens the bell to his loins by means of a strap or handkerchief.

The others are blindfolded, and placed at a certain distance, in a circle, from the jingler. As soon as he moves, the bell rings, and all rush forward and try to catch him. His business is to elude them, which he does by every means in his power; and, if he can avoid being caught for ten minutes, he has the prize; if not, the man who takes him becomes the jingler in turn, and so on, until one succeeds in baffling his pursuers for the required space of time. The fun consists in the blunders which the blinded make, in running against and catching one another instead of the bell-man; and in tumbling over obstacles that he throws in their way. The more they are baffled the more the people laugh and enjoy the sport.

When this was ended, the running in sacks commenced; and when the victor had received his reward, a space of an hour was allowed to those of the wrestlers who had joined in other sports, to recover their wind, previously to entering the ring to decide the most important part of the day's sport.

Julian Bachell, while the pig was chased, had contrived to speak a few words with the mediciner on the subject of the warning which Jansen had put into his hands; he learnt from him, that he had received an intimation from a trusty messenger, that the Bailiff of Dunster, a sort of chief constable, a man of a sour temper and much addicted to puritanism, had given out that he should call in the civil power to aid him in saving the temple of the Lord—meaning Culbone church—from the profanations of sinners. He added, that he marvelled he had not yet put his threats into execution.

Nothing however occurred to prevent the sports going on. Some were engaged in throwing the and winter livelihood, was very active, and led his pursuers a dance that they did not forget for many a day. After being chased for nearly an hour, he fairly gave them the slip, and they returned to the green with torn clothes and wounded limbs, to be laughed at by their friends.

Then came on the jingling-match, which is thus played. Six men toss up which of them shall first bear the bell; he upon whom the lot falls strips to the waist, and fastens the bell to his loins by means of a strap or handkerchief.

The others are blindfolded, and placed at a certain distance, in a circle, from the jingler. As soon as he moves, the bell rings, and all rush forward and try to catch him. His business is to elude them, which he does by every means in his power; and, if he can avoid being caught for ten minutes, he has the prize; if not, the man who takes him becomes the jingler in turn, and so on, until one succeeds in baffling his pursuers for the required space of time. The fun consists in the blunders which the blinded make, in running against and catching one another instead of the bell-man; and in tumbling over obstacles that he throws in their way. The more they are baffled the more the people laugh and enjoy the sport.

When this was ended, the running in sacks commenced; and when the victor had received his reward, a space of an hour was allowed to those of the wrestlers who had joined in other sports, to recover their wind, previously to entering the ring to decide the most important part of the day's sport.

Julian Bachell, while the pig was chased, had contrived to speak a few words with the medieiner on the subject of the warning which Jansen had put into his hands; he learnt from him, that he had received an intimation from a trusty messenger, that the Bailiff of Dunster, a sort of chief constable, a man of a sour temper and much addicted to puritanism, had given out that he should call in the civil power to aid him in saving the temple of the Lord—meaning Culbone church—from the profanations of sinners. He added, that he marvelled he had not yet put his threats into execution.

Nothing however occurred to prevent the sports going on. Some were engaged in throwing the

bar and putting the stone; others amused themselves by playing at quoits ; while the majority,
among whom were Julian Bachell and Hugh and
de Mohun, joined the merry dance around the
minstrels, having each selected a pretty country
lass as a partner. The morris-dancers mingled with
the rest, and, by the jingling of their bells, added
to the noise, if not to the merriment of the scene.

At a given signal, the wrestlers left their tent,
and took their stations near the stage. Master
Richard Luckes was appointed umpire, and the
first pair of combatants mounted. The defeated
man retired and another took his place, until six
had contended, and one was left conqueror. All
this occupied much time, and excited great interest. Every fall was attended with loud shouts from
the victor's friends, and he who remained the conqueror at last, was greeted with universal plaudits.

The shouts, however, were hushed when Alloway mounted the stage, and, throwing off his upper
coat, called in a loud voice for the Dunster student to come forth and try the best of three falls
with him.

Hugh sprung up to meet his adversary, already prepared for the struggle. Giles Tudball, Will Bowering, Master Jenkins, and the doctor, with his man Jansen, stood close to the platform, by the side of the wrestlers who had retired from it, to be ready in case of any foul play being meditated. Julian was on the opposite side, near some of his father's tenantry and servants, to whom he meant to appeal if their aid was required.

Master Alloway had been drinking more than he was aware of, and the liquor, and a sense of his former disgrace, added to the taunts of friends and foes, had put him in a very bad humour. He resolved not to shew any mercy to his young foe, but to rush in upon him, and if possible disable him from trying a second fall.

Hugh was cool and collected, and smiled, as he presented himself for the struggle, at the evident ill-temper of the butcher. Not a word was spoken; as they grappled, Hugh tried to shift his arms and grasp Alloway round the waist, to throw him over his hips, but the butcher, knowing how he had been defeated before, anticipated the movement, and succeeded in raising Hugh from the ground. He lifted him up high in the air and would have dashed him furiously to the earth and fallen on him, had not Hugh clasped his thighs so closely with his legs, that he caused him to stagger, and both came to the ground together.

" A fall, a fair fall!" shouted the wrestlers and the friends of Minehead.

" No fall, no fall, both down together," cried the Dunster men and the majority, who were evidently in favour of the youthful student.

" By G—d it was a fair fall!" cried the six wrestlers pressing towards the stage.

" Stand back—fair play—let the umpire decide," said Giles Tudball and his friends, placing themselves between the stage and the wrestlers, who, seeing that preparations were made to resist their interference, shouted to Master Luches to decide.

" No fall," said the umpire, amidst loud shouts.

The combatants again grappled, and the butcher threw out all his strength to overcome Hugh, who, like a pliant willow twig, gave way only to spring back again, until, watching his opportunity, he, with a slight touch of his foot, tripped up his rival and threw him from him on his back.

" A fair fall!" said the umpire.

" Take time, Master Alloway," said Hugh, " to recover your breath."

"I will take nothing of you but my revenge," said the butcher, staggering to his place and again grappling with Hugh, who, without giving him a moment's time, slipped from his hold, and, seizing him round the waist, threw him heavily over his hip upon the turf.

" The second fair fall, and the best of three!" from the umpire, was greeted with louder shouts from all but the regular wrestlers, who looked at each other and growled their dissatisfaction.

Again the combatants, at the earnest prayer of the defeated man, stood opposite to each other, and had just grasped elbow and collar, when a cir-cumstance, which must be recorded in another chapter, put a premature end to the interesting struggle.

CHAPTER VI.

THE crowd, who were gazing on in deep silence around the wrestlers' ring, and anxiously waiting for the players to commence the last good-naturedly conceded trial of skill and strength, were suddenly roused by a stentorian voice, calling to them, in the name of the Parliament of England, to abstain from forbidden sports and pastimes.

They turned to look at the speaker, and saw a tall gaunt figure dressed in a sort of half military suit of shabby leather. He wore a rusty breastplate over his chest, and an iron cap, fastened under his chin by a leathern thong, upon his head. In his right hand he carried a long pike tipped with steel, and in his left he held what seemed to be a parchment writing. By his side walked a thin reazenfaced man, clad in a suit of dark brown, with a short cloak of a sad colour, on his shoulders, and a high-peaked felt hat with an enormous breadth of brim, upon his head. His hair was closely cropped, and made his ears appear of an unnatural size; upon his neck was a broad falling collar, and upon his shrivelled legs a pair of large, loose, calf-skin boots; his right hand was supported by a strong crutch-headed stick, and under his left arm he carried a large black-bound bible, whose covers were kept together with a pair of enormous silver clasps.

Behind this pair of strange-looking figures, followed six men, dressed and armed like their gaunt leader, and casting sour and morose glances upon the assembled revellers.

They had approached close to the crowd without being observed, and made their way to the stage without opposition. Hugh de Mohun and Master Alloway, relaxed the hold they had taken of each other, and turned to gaze on the cause which had interrupted their play.

" Hugh de Mohun, pupil of the half papist priest of Dunster, and you, Master Alloway of Minehead,

leave off your ungodly wrestlings with the fleshly
arm, and come down from your unlawful pre-emi-
nence," shouted the tall leader, as he threw one of
his long legs upon the turf, and raised himself to
the platform by the aid of his pike.

"Who is he that dares stop our sports?" said
some of the crowd.

"It is Master Roger Priver, the wool-comber of
Dunster, who claims to be high bailiff of the town,"
cried some Dunster men.

"And who is that little scarecrow, that hath
crawled up to the stage in his rear?"

"That is Master Robert Browne, who writeth
himself reverend, and who was turned out of his pulpit in Dunster church, for preaching strange doctrines."

"Is he come here to preach to us, think you?"

"I doubt it not, for see, he is preparing to open
his battery: he is unclasping his black book."

Hugh de Mohun placed his cap on his head, and,
folding his arms across his chest, gazed calmly in
Master Priver's face. Alloway, laying aside all
feelings of animosity, stood by his late foe, to support him, if necessary, against the civil force.

"Down I say, young man, and depart in peace, lest a worse thing befall thee," shouted Master Roger," and thou, butcher, get thee home to thy shambles, lest thy body be converted into as worthless a carcass as one of the rotten sheep that thou sometimes cheatest thy customers withal."

"Thou liest! thou snivelling wool-tearer--"

"Nay Master Alloway, speak him fair," said Hugh; "by what authority, Master Roger Priver, are you here to interrupt our innocent amusements?"

"Innocent! sayest thou? soul-destroying, carnal, devilish—" began the puritan priest.

"Hush, Master Browne, hush!" said the bailiff, "waste not thy words on such as he. I am here, Hugh de Mohun, in mine office as high bailiff of Dunster, deputed by—"

"Thou art not high bailiff. Master Thomas Luttrell, by virtue of his rights as lord of the manor of Dunster, and a lieutenant of the county, did depose thee from thine office for illegally supporting the recreant priest there in his heterodoxy. He hath his rights from the king."

"King me no king, bold boy, I am appointed to

mine office by the parliament, whose power is above the king's."

Not yet I trow, Master Roger, though the round-headed knaves begin to express their disaffection and disloyalty a little too openly. We, of the loyal county of Somerset, care not for the parliament; we obey our lawful sovereign, King Charles."

"Long live King Charles, and down with the puritan parliament!" shouted the crowd. "Fell the wool-comber to the ground, butcher, and you, Master Hugh, toss the snuffling preacher over to our tender mercies."

The six bailiff's men, thinking their captain in danger, mounted the stage and took their places by his side; at the same time, Julian Bachell, Giles Tudball, and several others, among whom were the wrestlers, one by one gained the stage, and ranged themselves near their friends.

"Down, down, I say to thee, Hugh de Mohun," cried Roger Priver, "or I will strike thee with my pike."

Hugh felt for his pistols, forgetting that he had taken them from his belt and given them into the

care of Doctor Graveboys, before he began to con-
tend in the wrestling match.

Roger Priver saw the motion, and understood
the meaning of it. " Ah, ah !" he cried, " would'st
use carnal arms against the deputed officer of the
parliament? down I say, or I will strike thee."

As he spoke, he lowered the handle of his pike,
meaning to strike the haft of it on the ground; but
it unfortunately lighted, but not lightly, on the
foot of butcher Alloway, who, stung with the pain
and the disasters of the day, struck the bailiff a
blow in the face, which would have stretched his
body on the turf, had he not been caught in his fall
and supported by his men.

" Curses light on thee!" shouted the bailiff, " lay
on my men—cut, slay, and destroy."

" Hew them down—cut into pieces the men of
Belial, even as Samuel hewed Agag," cried the
preacher.

" Down with the clothier loons, whose hands are
more suited to the shuttle than the spear," shouted
the crowd as they rushed towards the stage.

A few blows were exchanged, and a general fight

would have ensued, had not the pikes been wrested from the hands of Roger Priver and his followers, and Julian Bachell, aided by Hugh de Mohun, done all he could by word and deed to prevent bloodshed.

Still the crowd pressed on, and the platform was filled. Roger Priver, seeing that he was protected by the two young men, drew forth his commission, and a proclamation from the parliament forbidding the holding of wakes, fairs, revels, and all sorts of junketings. He read the contents at the top of his loud voice, but his words were drowned by the hissings, hootings, and revilings of the crowd : at last, just as he was finishing the long, wordy proclamation, butcher Alloway snatched the parchment from his hand, and, in the midst of loud hurrahs, tore it into pieces, and scattered the shreds amongst the crowd below.

Again a fight had nearly ensued, for the bailiff was not deficient in courage, and made a rush at Alloway, to recover his much-prized warrant of service. Julian and Hugh, however, seized him each by one of his long bony arms, and begged him not to risk his life by his rashness.

"I care not for life, tear me limb from limb an you list; I will have my own. Woe, woe, he hath torn my warrant into shreds—Ichabod! Ichabod! my glory hath departed."

"Gag the canting thief"—cried Giles Tudball, "or we shall have bloodshed."

"Silence," cried Julian "silence, my friends! let them depart in peace, and let us resume our sports."

"And who art thou that would'st dictate to us, Sir Forester," cried one of the crowd. "Better seek thy hut in Exmoor, and look after thy bucks and does."

"Hush," said one near him, a fair-haired girl, "thou knowest not whom thou insultest, and would'st give thy tongue a bite, ere thou said'st wrong of the seeming forester."

"And who is the mummer then, wench?"

"Thy master's son, Julian Bachell," said the girl in a whisper, "and may your lands be taken from you, and your farm be given to another, if you do not see that he suffer no wrong."

The man left his place, and sought his brother

tenants, to whom he communicated the news he
had just learnt. They gathered together in a body,
and forced their way to the stage, to be ready to assist their young master, if he should appear to
need their help.

"Silence: I entreat you to hear me," cried
Julian.

"Hear him not—hear him not—he will se-
duce you with words of man's wisdom," cried the
preacher, "listen rather to me, and I will expose to
you your wickedness, and show unto you on what
a broken reed you are leaning. In the book of
Numbers, chapter—" but his words were drowned
in the shouts of the crowd, who called to those on
the platform to kill the high bailiff and his clothier loons, and to pull out the false priest's wag-
ging tongue.

"To Tophet shall you go—to Tophet—lo! the
fire is kindled, put on more thorns—heap on the
wood—make it hot—"shouted the preacher, "truly
into the pit shall ye be hurled—ye shall go down
below—"

"Nay rather," said Master Jenkins, "*you* shall

go down below, for I will save thee in spite of thyself from the fate that will befall thee, if thou ut-
terest thy follies and threats to the irritated crowd."

The Welshman placed his left hand upon the
priest's mouth, and taking him under his right arm,
bore him, struggling and kicking with all his
might and main, into the wood beyond the crowd,
where he strapped him to a tree by his belt, and
left him with his cloak tied round his head, to
preach through its thick folds to the trees and
tethered horses.

While this was going on, Master Roger Priver,
who was held tightly by the young men, turned
to Julian, and inquired who he was that dared
to oppose the authority of parliament by confining
the person of their deputed officer.

"It matters not who I am ; I am anxious to
prevent the murder of your men, and to save your
life, if you will only listen to and follow my advice," said Julian.

"Thou slayer of deer and trainer of dogs, thou
bloodhound, who huntest after those who would
take the wild beasts of the forest, which were made

"Th

for the use of all men! I will not listen to such as thou art, but will wrestle with thee even to the death."

Roger, as he said this, foaming at the mouth like a maniac, suddenly withdrew his arm, and struck Julian a severe blow.

" A Bachell, a Bachell ! to the rescue," shouted the man to whom the lodge-keeper's daughter had given the information that it was his young master, who, disguised as a forester, was taking so prominent a part in the proceedings of the day.

" Ah ! ah ! a Bachell," cried the excited bailiff, who was still held by Hugh de Mohun. " A Bachell is it?—spawn of a tyrant, thy father shall rue this day."

" To the rescue!" cried the tenants and servants of Ashley Combe, and like a wave they surged forward in a body, and filled the platform.

" Back—back—I intreat you, blood will flow else. I am not hurt," cried Julian.

" We will not back, until we have paid the insolent wool-comber for the blow."

" Nay, nay, hurt him not; take away his followers, and see them safe from the crowd, if you love me; we will manage the bailiff, who is already held securely by my friend and Giles Tudball; away with them, and use them not ill."

The men obeyed the former part of their young master's wishes, and seized the bailiff's followers, who offered no resistance, but permitted themselves to be dragged through the crowd, who jeered, hissed, and shouted at them as they passed to the spot where the preacher had been conveyed by Master Jenkins. There, however, the latter part of Julian's orders was not attended to; for they bound them with their faces to the trees, and administered to each and all of them a sound drubbing, with some stout hazel wands and young ground-ashes, which they cut for the purpose.

"Here, Will, where art thou man?" shouted Giles Tudball.

"Here, at your starboard elbow, captain," replied Will.

"Thou art good at a running-knot, give two turns of your belt round this babbler's mouth, and make it fast behind; he will not stow his talk, while the lee-scuppers of his mouth remain open."

" In the name of the parl—" began Roger Priver, but ere he could finish the terrible threat, the
belt was passed twice over his mouth, and he finished in dumb-show, dancing with wrath so vigorously, that it changed the anger of the crowd to
mirth.

" To the brook with him!—duck him, duck him!
the cold water will cure his rage," cried Master
Richard Luckes, who doubtless felt assured in his
mind that the bailiff's interference with the sports
would greatly diminish the profits of his booth.

" To the brook—to the brook!" shouted the
crowd, and in spite of all Julian and Hugh could do,
Master Roger Priver was seized by the people
nearest, and hurried off to the brook, where he
was laid at the bottom of the stream, and turned
over and over until he was well nigh drowned.

" Enough, enough, you will murder him,"
shouted Hugh.

" And a good thing too—he deserves it; but we
will save him for another fate; he will be sure to
be hanged some day," said Giles Tudball, who thus
made the crowd laugh, and probably saved the fellow's life.

" The preacher, the preacher! let us duck the preacher! He must needs be dry—dry as his own discourses," cried the crowd; and a rush was made towards the spot where the deposed minister was tied, and still uttering anathemas in the dark against his persecutors.

Before they could reach the spot, they were arrested in their career by an extraordinary noise. All the horses and ponies that were tethered to the trees in the wood, set up a loud and prolonged neighing, and were replied to by other horses who seemed to be coming down the combe.

" Even the dumb animals are laughing to think how rightly the knaves have been served," said Giles Tudball.

" It strikes me that they are putting a veto on the proceedings, by saying *neigh* to them," said the mediciner's man, who stood by Hugh and Julian and laughed loudly at his own wit.

The neighing ceased, and as the crowd were silent, the heavy tread as of a body of horse was heard coming down the hard, rocky path beside the brook. In a few minutes, a tall elderly man

dressed in a horseman's suit of dark grey, with a
cloak, falling collar, and large steeple-crowned hat,
a huge rapier called a tuck at his side, and a large
pair of pistols at his saddle-bow, rode from under
the trees, followed by a troop of soldiers, to the
number of twenty, and all heavily armed.

"Who are these?" asked Hugh de Mohun.

"As I live," cried the mediciner, "it is Master
John Pym. I know him well, for I have seen
him oft in his own borough of Tavistock—away,
away!—Giles Tudball, your boat is in readiness,
give me and my man Jansen a cast to Minehead.
Come, young sir, and you Will Bowering follow me;
no time must be lost; through the wood here,
where they cannot follow us without dismounting."

So saying, Dr. Graveboys dashed into the cop-
pice, and led the way to the cove of Culbone, followed by Giles Tudball and the rest of the party.
Julian was anxious to find his way home through
the woods, but was dissuaded by Hugh de Mohun
and Giles Tudball, who offered to land him at
Porlock-wear.

A breeze was blowing from the westward, the

wind having chopped round during the day, as if to favor their escape; and a few minutes saw the lug-sails set with every reef shaken out, and the Blossom of Minehead running before the wind. and with the tide in her favour.

"We are well out of his clutches," said the doctor, as they sailed along.

"Nay *we* can hardly be said to be safe, though *you* may be," said Julian.

"Well, never mind," said Hugh, "do not let us be melancholy—come Giles, strike up a merry song."

Giles complied at once, and trolled forth

THE BOATMAN'S SONG.

Spread wide to the winds the fluttering sails,
　Bid the masts the strong gales defy;
The heart of the mariner never quails,
　Who relies for protection on high.

CHORUS.

With good canvass aloft, and stout oak below
What fear we my messmates where'er we go!

Our loved ones at home watch our craft from the shore,
   As the treacherous billows we dare ;
And we fear not the wave's tempestuous roar,
   For they raise for our safety a prayer.

                 With, &c.

Then court the fierce winds for our gallant boat,
   She will skim o'er the waves like a bird ;
And when in our haven we quietly float,
   They will know that their prayers were heard.

                 With, &c.

This song was followed by many more, ere Julian
Bachell leapt ashore at the wear of Porlock ; and,
bidding farewell to his friends, sought the Lodge
of Ashley Combe.

CHAPTER VII.

MASTER Luckes, the harbour-master of the port of Minehead, had been left by his son in charge of the Ship-aground, while he and his spouse were absent at the revels at Culbone. Knowing the old gentleman's propensity for indulging in strong waters, his daughter-in-law had left him a half-pint of brandy for his own drinking, locked the cupboard in which the spirits were kept, and taken the key with her.

Master Luckes was not long in getting through his modicum, for he had but little else to do but to sit, and sip, and smoke his pipe. Most of the customers of the little hostelry were either gone to the revel, or were too busy in their respective occupations to find time for sitting and soaking in an

alehouse.   The brandy being finished, and, having
nothing else to do, for he could not endure a dry
pipe, Master Luckes threw himsef back in a huge
leather-covered chair and fell fast asleep, after he
had warned the wench who was chambermaid, boots,
waitress, and even ostler upon occasion, to keep a
sharp look-out, and rouse him if a customer came in.
Mabel watched him till she saw he was sound
asleep, and then tripped lightly across the street
to the quay to have a little talk with her sweetheart, the mate of the St. David, who was busy in
unlading her cargo, in the absence of Master Jenkins, his skipper.

How long Master Luckes had been asleep, he did
not know, when he was roused by a deep-toned
melodious voice calling in his ear, " What ho ! harbour-master, art dead ? or have your potations been
so deep as to produce a lethargy ?"

" Mabel—ye pest—Mabel ye good-for-naught,"
cried the old man not turning round in his chair,
" hear ye not? a customer calleth for ale.   Mix it
wench, for the big tun runneth somewhat hard
and stale."

"Mabel, man, like the rest of the gadabouts of Minyead is off for the junketings at Culbone, I believe; and here have I been wasting my lungs in calling house, until I was weary, and was about to leave what I thought a deserted place, when I saw thy lean carcass ensconced in the chair; rouse thee man!"

"Mabel, Mabel, where is the jade?" cried the old man.

"Out, I tell thee; gone a-junketing like her master and mistress. Thou art parcel-drunk, harbour-master, and hast been drinking the strong waters thyself in lack of customers."

"Who says that?" said the old man, looking round sharply, "who dares to say that I would defraud any one, letting alone mine own son? Ah, Master Robert Quirke, I do demand your forgiveness; I was somewhat sleepy and overcome with much business."

"With much liquor, more likely. Your eyes bear proof that your lips and the goblet have been too intimately acquainted."

"I have tasted but one half-pint all the day,

Master Quirke; I am an ill-used man for—would you believe it?—Richard's wife hath turned key on the spirit-cupboard, and left me not the means of solacing myself with a cordial, or of supplying such as you with aught but cider or ale, which are wont to cause a coldness of stomach."

"I would taste your ale, Master Luckes, which is wont to be good," said the stranger, taking a seat.

"Good enough, I trow, for ale—but still chilly to an aged stomach. Mabel, I say, what Mabel!"

"You are wasting much of the little breath you have left; Mabel I tell you is gone, like the rest, a-revelling."

"Nay, I am here sir," said Mabel, who on seeing a customer enter the inn, had left her sweetheart, run round into the house by the back-door, and now made her appearance with a platter in one hand and a cloth in the other, to make the locum tenens of her master and mistress believe, that she had been busily engaged in the duties of the pantry.

"Where hast been, wench, that thou didst not answer when I called so long and loudly?"

"I cried 'coming' but I could not leave my work at a moment's warning," said the girl; "but you grow deaf, and the brandy you drank made you sleep heavily."

"Brandy! ye ne'er do well; thou knowest—but what boots it to complain to such as thou? down into the cellar, girl, and draw for Master Robert Quirke of the best."

The girl obeyed and returned with a full quart into which she put a bit of toasted bread and grated a little ginger and nutmeg, and then handed it to the guest, who took a deep draught before he passed it to the harbour-master. The old man smelt it, and put it down from his mouth, his resolution not to taste of it, however, failed him; and, after a few words upon the coldness and unwholesomeness of it to aged stomachs, he raised it to his lips and drained it to the dregs.

Master Quirke smiled, as he filled his pipe, and bade Mabel prepare a second quart, and spice it well, lest it should disagree with Master Luckes. The old man did not like the smile, and, fearing that he should have a lecture on his well-known failing, to turn away the guest's attention, expressed his surprise that he had not been to the revel.

"Revels, Master Enckes, I have done with. I am an old man like yourself, though my hand trembles not, and my legs are not swollen; for I have shunned aught in the way of drink but good wholesome ale. I have been a fortunate man; and though I have worked hard through calm and storm as a mariner, I have escaped the dangers of the deep. I would show my gratitude to heaven, by leaving some portion of the riches which I have accumulated for the benefit of my fellowmen."

"Folks say that Master Quirke is building a mansion for himself in the town, on the acres he hath bought of Squire Luttrell," said the harbourmaster.

"I am building; but not for myself, Master Luckes. Folks say wrong if they report that I design to build a mansion to dwell in."

"What mean then the cargoes of stone and lime, and timber, that pay the duties of the harbour, and are all consigned to Robert Quirke."

" I tell thee, man, I am building ; but not for my-self, and when I have closed this door that Ma-bel's sharp ears may not be benefited, I will reveal to thee what no mortal has ever yet heard."

When Master Quirke had closed the door, he took his seat by the fire again, and, after a deep draught of the replenished jack, disclosed his secret thus :

"Thou knowest, Master Luckes, that when Mistress Leckey died some ten years since, she told her son, who used to freight vessels here, and trade to Waterford, that she would appear upon earth again, and grant him a wind which he might have whistled for in vain."

" I know it well," said the old man.

"But you do not know that I believed not in the tale, but even scoffed at it, and assigned the ruin of Tom Leckey to his fondness for the goblet and the can, rather than to the tricks and whims of his dead mother. I have laughed when they told me of her pranks on shore and at sea."

" Ah, I have heard thee, I have heard thee, in this very room, Master Quirke, jeer at the pottycarrier when he told thee that Dame Leckey, the grey woman of Minyead, had beaten him black and blue with her crutched stick, because he failed to help her ghostship over a stile."

" I did laugh, and should laugh even now at so improbable a story, Master Luckes, had I not seen and heard her myself."

" As how?" said the harbour-master, looking round, as if afraid of seeing the grey woman at his elbow, and assailing the ale-jack to give him courage.

" It was on a dreary night, this last December. I had been over to Swansea, with a cargo of goods, and was returning with a freight of wools for the Dunster clothiers. My crew were asleep below, and I was alone on deck, standing near the tiller. It was a dead calm, and I had taken a double turn of the starboard guy-rope, and made it fast to the tiller, to keep the ship's head steady in the tide; and, as I smoked my pipe, and whistled now and then for a wind to waft me up Channel and into harbour, I heard of a sudden as it were the flap of wings, and something passed close to me which looked like a large sea-gull; it sailed up aloft,

and settled on the mast-head. I should have accounted it to be some scared sea-mew, for it whistled loud and shrill, had I not known that the web-
bed feet of such birds, are all unfitted for lighting
on 'a dog-vane. Well, harbour-master, there it
sat, and whistled so shrilly, that its cry might
have been heard at Cardiff, as it seemed to me.
Suddenly, the wind arose and filled the mainsail,
so that the vessel lay over on her side, and the
foaming waters rushed over the gunwale and
flooded her deck. I was fain to haul up the main-
tack, and to shout to the crew below. No one
answered to my call. I looked aloft, and there sat
the same grey figure, but, instead of the whistling
which I before heard, the sound of gibes and laughter reached my ear, amidst the rattling of the top-
gear and the creaking of ropes and blocks. I
was an angered, Master Luckes, and in my anger
I swore and used profane words, and told the bird,
as I thought it, if he were the devil himself and
would alight on the deck, I would do his bidding
whatever it might be."

"T'was rash language, Master Quirke, and I

doubt not, no good came of it," said the harbour-
master.

" I had scarce spoken the words, when the figure
sprung lightly from the mast-head, and stood before
me on the deck. The binnacle light showed me
the visage of a grey woman, that is a woman dressed in a grey suit, such as Mistress Leckey of
Minyead ever wore. I could see through her
form, Master Luckes, the mast and the cordage, and
the main hatchway before which she stood. I
would have spoken to her, but, somehow or other,
my tongue refused its office, and my throat felt as
though I had swallowed hot coals. I could only
gaze on her, and, though the wind blew louder than
any hurricane in the Western Indies, and the waves
roared and splashed against the vessel's sides, I heard
these words as distinctly as if the dead calm, which
I had been whistling to dispel, had continued:

> ' Thou hast but one son and never a spouse
>   To inherit thy hard-earn'd gains;
>   Build for the poor a goodly almshouse,
>   It will save thee of hell the pains.' "

" And what followed—did she disappear in blue
flames and leave the smell of brimstone behind

her?" said Master Luckes, scarcely above his breath.

"I cannot tell you; I was roused as from a deep sleep by my crew, whom the rolling of the ship, and the wash of the waves against her clinker-built sides, had brought upon deck. I said nothing of what I had seen and heard; but, as we rushed before the wind up Channel, and made our port, I vowed to Heaven to comply with the commands so fearfully sent to me. I bought a piece of land overright the market-house of good Master Luttrell, and am building what I hope may prove a quiet resting-place for those who may be in need and necessity, for centuries after I am dead and gone."

"Did you not consult the parson?" said Master Euckes.

"I did not; such was my intention, but, as you know Master Robert Browne of Dunster had unsettled men's minds; and our patron was gone to Bath to lay complaints against him before the Bishop, and to have the good Master Snelling inducted in his room. I kept my counsel, therefore, and though I believe that what I saw and heard was but a dream, I am not sorry that I resolved to act upon it. But you will keep my secret, Master Luckes, until I am dead and gone ?"

" Ay, will I indeed, though in truth 'tis a marvellous tale and worthy recording."

" What, ho ! within there ! house, I say !" cried a shrill voice, which made Master Luckes nearly spring from his seat.

" Bah! man, never be frightened. It is the cry of •Master Basil Chipera, the parish-clerk and cordwainer of Dunster," said Master Quirke.

" And what brings him here I wonder ?" said the temporary landlord, as the individual named opened the door and entered the room.

" As good a forest pony as ever was foaled on Exmoor, Master Luckes," said a little, shrivelled figure, dressed in a suit of iron-grey. " Here are rare doings, my masters, up at Dunster, I trow."

" What news dost bring ?" inquired Robert Quirke.

" Here hath been a half-score horsemen of the new militia raised by Master John Pym, to speer after master Hugh de Mohun, whom they accuse of revelling and rioting in an ungodly manner at Culbone."

" Is he not at home then ?" inquired the cunning old harbour-master.

" Thou knowest very well, Master Luckes, that he donned his mumming dress, and went away this morning early in the Blossom of Minyead with Giles Tudball. There has been it seems, an attack made upon Master Robert Browne, Roger Priver and his constables, who would have been foully murdered, had not Master Pym ridden over Dunkery hill and been at hand in time to save them," said Basil Chipera.

" And what business had the like of them at Culbone ?" asked the old man.

" Roger Priver, had it seems, authority from the parliament to put a stop to the revels, but not having a warrant from Master Thomas Luttrell, who is away to fetch his ward, no one would obey him, and Master Alloway and your son Richard and others, have got themselves into trouble, and are under arrest."

" And Hugh de Mohun ?" inquired Master Luckes.

"Is escaped with Giles Tudball, Will Bowering, and the mediciner, whom you know as Dr. Grave-boys. The soldiers await his return to Dunster Castle, and I, whom they shut up in the upper room of the gateway, made bold to slip down, as doth Master Hugh, by means of the ivy-stems, and mount my pony and gallop down here, to give him warning of his danger."

"And what says good parson Snelling, thy master and the boy's tutor?" said Robert Quirke.

"He is nigh distraught. He has been wondering all day where his charge might be, and many lies have I been obliged to invent to account for his absence; but what is to be done? if he comes up to Dunster he will be arrested, and the Lord knows what may be the upshot of it."

"Do you return to Dunster, Master Basil, and leave the young man to me. Take a draught of ale, and hie thee back to comfort the good parson," said Robert Quirke.

It was growing dark when the parish clerk of Dunster remounted his forest pony and gallop-ed along the quay. Robert Quirke, as soon as he was fairly out of sight, descended the steps of the pier, and, getting into a boat, rowed off to the head of the harbour, whence he could get a view of any vessel rounding Greenaleigh point and steering for Minehead. His practised eye soon detected the lugger of Giles Tudball coming up Channel, and he pulled vigorously to get to her side before she tacked to run into the harbour.

CHAPTER VIII.

WE must leave Master Robert Quirke, to wait
for the coming. up of the Blossom of Minehead,
while we return to the scene of Culbone revel.

No sooner had the soldiers, with Master John
Pym at their head, taken possession of the ground
lately occupied by the revellers, than most of those
assembled followed the example set them by the
mediciner and Giles Tudball, and made the best
of their way to their respective homes, for fear of
consequences, which, being unknown, appeared
doubly fearful.

Master Pym, stationing himself as nearly as he
could in the middle of the green, close to the raised
platform, drew from his pocket a piece of parch-

ment, bearing a twin-like resemblance to the skin carried by the bailiff, Roger Priver, which Alloway had torn into shreds. He opened it deliberately, and, as he held it closely to his eyes, which some sixty years' use had rendered somewhat weak, the better to read its contents, the said bailiff, dripping with wet and exhausted by the ill-usage he had met with, laid his hand upon his knee, and begged him to seize the transgressors of the law, before they could make their escape.

" Not so, good bailiff, I will not follow their example, but will proceed legally. I was bred to the bar, and require not to be taught my duty ; did I not impeach Buckingham and Mainwaring, and conduct and bring to a happy issue the trial of the Lord Strafford ? and have I not successfully resisted the illegal attempt of Charles Stuart, to arrest me and four other members of the parliament, within the house of Commons ? Back good Master Priver, and let me not, I pray thee, said John Pym, in a voice drawlingly slow, but firm.

" Nay but Master Pym, I would avenge myself on mine adversaries whiles they are in the way with

me," said the bailiff. "Have I not had my commission stolen from me, been roughly handled, and
well-nigh suffocated in the waters that overwhelm-
ed me ? Have not my men been maltreated, and,
with the pious and God-fearing Master Browne,
been tied to trees and beaten with ashen boughs?
I would avenge me and mine."

"Take four of my troop, and release the divine
and thy companions, and if, when I have read the
order of the parliament in the ears of the people,
any of the malcontents become captives to thy
spear and thy bow, thou mayest arrest them, but
leave the law to punish them : 'Vengeance is mine,'
thou knowest the rest."

Roger Priver did as he was ordered, and while, he
went to releaese the unfortunate posse comitatus
and the deposed minister, Master Pym read in slow
and solomn tones, a long rigmarole, couched in the
puritanical and half blasphemous style of the age,
against, 'wakes, revels, junketings, church-ales,
bride-ales, and such-like ungodly sports.' His only
hearers were his soldiery, who, with solemn visages
and upturned eyes, pronounced a sonorous snuf-

fling Amen, as he concluded and folded up the proclamation.

The only parties who had not fled were Master Richard Luckes, his wife, and Alloway, who,
while the proclamation was being read, were hastily
dismantling the tent or drinking-booth, and hurrying their goods as fast as they could into the boat of
Master Jenkins, who was waiting for them in the
cove. No sooner, however, had Roger Priver un-
bound his captive officers and the preacher, than he
strode hastily across the green, followed by Master
Pym and the soldiers, and commenced an attack
upon the canvass tent which was speedily torn into
tatters and rent in twain, as the preacher said, like
the veil which hid the Scheckinah from the eyes of
the Israelites.

Master Luckes and the butcher resisted manfully, but were soon overpowered, and bound tightly with sword-belts to trees. Mrs. Luckes amused
herself by alternately sobbing and abusing her enemies in good set terms to the horror of the divine,
who undertook to convince her, in a sermon of sixteen
heads, that she was nought but a modern Jezabel.

Master Jenkins, seeing his friends in captivity, and knowing that his single arm could not release them loosed his boat and pushed off from shore.

As soon as the tent was demolished, an attack was made on its contents, the spigots were torn from the barrels, and beer and cider flowed forth in streams; the casks themselves were next demolished with the aid of quoits and throwing-bars; and the bottles containing the strong waters would have shared their fate, had not some one suggested to Roger Priver that his immersion in the brook might prove dangerous to him, unless he took something as a preventive of cold.

Roger took the hint and the preventive, in a copious draught from a squat bottle; an example that was followed by every one of the party, although they took it in so solemn a manner, and with such sour looks, that a spectator might have fancied they were swallowing one of Master Graveboy's most nauseous specifics, instead of right good Scheidam or pure Dantzic. The bottles, having been emptied, were broken to pieces, and the party looked round for some other abomination whereon to work destruction.   The only thing, however, that remained, was the gay hangings suspended from the oak by the minstrels, which, in their hurry and haste to escape, they had been unable to remove ; a few seconds saw them torn into shreds and scattered to the winds.

All this time Master John Pym stood by, viewing the scene with a solemn visage and not saying a word, although Mrs. Luckes was intreating him at the top of her lungs " to exert his authority and save her worldly goods," which did not in the least interfere with the exhortation of the divine, who had just got to " and seventhly" in his discourse, when the commander ordered his troops to fall in and Roger Priver to follow with the prisoners. Mistress Luckes was placed on her own pillion be- hind the preacher, who insisted upon this arrange- ment that he might conclude his sermon as they marched.   Her husband and Alloway were strap- ped each behind a trooper, with their hands secure- ly tied *en derrière.*

In this way they ascended the path, across the brook, down which Julian Bachell and Hugh de

Mohun had come in the morning. It was already getting dusk, and the branches which overhung them made the road dark and dangerous to be travelled; so that they proceeded but slowly, to enable those on foot to keep up with the horsemen.

Before they reached the summit of the first ascent, the horse, the property of Master Richard Luckes, on which the preacher and Mistress Luckes rode, commenced a series of gambols, a thing he was never known to do before; which ended in his stumbling over a huge stone, and pitching Master Browne over his head; much to the delight of its other rider, who kept her seat by clinging to her pillion, and quietly extracted the pin which she had inserted into the beast's skin, when she found her plan for ridding herself of the preacher had been successful. As nothing could induce the divine to mount again, he was obliged to shuffle after the horse, commencing his "thirteenthly" between his deep pantings as he best might.

"Forward, master high bailiᵹ," cried one of the soldiers, "Master Pym would confer with thee."

Roger Priver went to the head of the little band, and walked beside the leader's horse.

" Did I not understand thee to say, that the son of the malignant man Bachell, of Ashley Lodge hard by, was one of those who assaulted thee in thy duty?"

"Yea did I; he was mummed as a forester of Exmoor, and did use me grievously," said Roger Priver.

" He was leader doubtless in the ungodly pastimes?"

"Yea verily—that is to say joint-leader with the other springald who was disguised, as a seaman."

" What name doth he bear?"

" Hugh de Mohun; he dwelleth with Master Robert Snelling, who did dispossess good Master Browne of his pulpit, over the gateway of Dunster Castle, of which one Basil Chipera is warder and parish-clerk, for want of a better," said the bailiff.

" Countenanced in his disobedience by the surpliced priest and that other malignant who owneth Dunster, Master Thomas Luttrell, doubtless?"

" Thou speakest truly, and verily together they led the revels and the fray, and were the first to resist my authority, to tear up my credentials, and to give us up to the Philistines to be cruelly entreated."

" What more ? "

" The young Hugh would have drawn pistol on me but that he had resigned his weapons to some one, while he strove with the arm of flesh with the seller of flesh at Minyead. He also rolled me in the troubled waters of the brook, until my mortal soul had well-nigh quitted its earthly tabernacle," groaned out the lying bailiff.

" It shall be seen to, it shall be seen to, Master Priver ; in insulting thee, they have insulted the parliament. The herd may escape scathless, but the leaders thereof, bulls of Basan as they be, must be made an example to others, that they offend not again."

" Had we not better seize the whelp in his lair as we pass, and before he have notice of our coming and hide himself ? "

" Such is my intention ; I cross not Grabhurst hill to Cutcombe this night ; but will e'en refresh at Ashley Combe and secure the prisoner, and then ride on to Dunster where it shall be proved whether Master Luttrell, the owner of its strong Castle, will refuse to give hospitality to an officer of the parliament, and to deliver up into his hands the disciple of yon surpliced priest."

"Ahumph!" said Roger Priver, in a sort of grunt, which implied deep-felt satisfaction.

Nothing further was said, until they reached the spot where the road branches off to the Lodge. There, Master Pym ordered all his men but six to proceed to Dunster, with the constables and the prisoners. He kept the bailiff and the preacher with him, intending to supply them with horses from the Lodge stables, and to take them on with him, after he had refreshed his party and secured his prisoner.

In the mean while, Julian Bachell, who, as the reader may remember, had sailed round Bossington Point, with Hugh and the rest, in Giles Tudball's lugger, had arrived at his landing-place, about a quarter of an hour after Master Pym reached Ashley-Combe Lodge.

He stepped lightly ashore, and hurried over the rough stones of the beach towards the wear. Just as he was crossing the wear, a sort of rudely fashioned water-gate, which prevented the tide from receding from the basin and leaving it dry, he saw some one come out of one of the three fisher-men's huts which stood beside it. She, for it was a female, came towards him just as he was quitting the plank which served as a bridge.

"Back, Master Julian, back as you love your liberty," she said in a clear whisper, " enemies are at hand."

" Why, how now pretty Janet, what makes you here after dusk ? men must not have aught to say against my foster-sister, and when girls are out, like owls, at twilight, they are apt to gain the name of light o' loves," said Julian, kindly.

" I come, Master Julian," said the gate-keeper's daughter, " by my father's orders, though not un-willingly, for I care not what men say falsely of me, to warn you not to come up to the Lodge to-night."

" And why not ? surely my father—"

"He is not yet returned; but there is Master John Pym of Cutcombe, the enemy of all good and true men, up there, with Roger Priver, the preacher, and some troopers. They are searching for you, and have arrested the servants, and shut up my father in his own gate-house. I made bold to escape by the back window, and, as I knew you had sailed with Master Hugh and would land here, hurried down to warn you."

" Thanks, my good Janet, thanks—but who comes here?"

"A boy, and, as I think, the tapster-boy from the Blue Anchor," said Janet.

" What now boy, whom seek you thus stealthily?"

"An it please your honour, I seek yourself; good Mistress Luckes, whom the troopers are carrying prisoner to Ashley Combe, strapped to her pony, like a basket of chickens or a side of venison, whispered me, while the soldiers and constables took their bearer, to meet you and warn you not to go up to the Lodge to-night, but to put out in a boat and hail Master Jenkins, who will shortly round the headland on his way to Minyead."

" 'Tis well done of Mistress Luckes, and I will not forget to reward her; and now, Janet, do you go back to the Lodge, and secretly warn the serving-

men to offer no resistance, and if possible give my
father notice of all that has happened; away my
good girl, and good night.   The tapster here will
go with me, and bring the boat ashore when I am
safely seated with Master Jenkins."

Janet tripped off as soon as she had seen Julian
launch one of the small boats that lay on the beach,
and quickly mounted the steep path : when she
gained the Lodge-gate, she looked cautiously
round, and listened attentively ; neither seeing no
hearing anything to alarm her, she knocked at th
door, and whispered through the key-hole to her fa
ther, that Master Julian had left Porlock-wear fo
Minehead.   She then with more caution followe
the hard road which led up to the Lodge itself, un
til she came within view of the house.   Concealing
herself behind a large walnut tree, she endeavoure
to see what was going on within.   Lights were
burning in the great hall, and every now and ther
a shadow, as of one bearing refreshments, passe
over the large window.   Creeping behind the ever
greens that skirted the circular carriage-road, sh
sought the stables, where the horses were busily

eating the corn put before them, still saddled, and having their bridles thrown on their necks. Passing at the back of the stables, she gained the offices, and, mounting by a projection in the wall, looked into the large kitchen, where she saw two or three of the women seated and crying by the fire, while others, with the serving-men, were preparing dishes for the men in the hall.

Seeing that no soldiers or strangers were amongst them, Janet tapped smartly at the window, and could not help laughing at the effect produced by " the sound herself had made."   The servants set down the dishes they were about to carry in; those who were seated sprung up on their feet, and all, huddled together in the middle of the room, gazed with terror-fraught eyes at the window whence the unexpected sound proceeded.

She tapped again louder than before, and the servants huddled together more closely, clinging to each other for support, until one, bolder than the rest, left the group and approached the window.

" It is I—Janet; do not be afraid, but open the window." The man sprang on a sort of dresser, and opened the window, or rather four quarries of glass in an iron frame, formed for letting out heat and admitting air.

" Master Julian hath escaped; his orders are, that no resistance be offered to the intruders, but that they have all that they demand," said Janet.

" It needs not Master Julian's orders to insure that; for the knaves have seized on everything without the asking, and are sitting cheek by jowl, gentle and simple, higglety-pigglety at the same table, eating and drinking as though they meant to pay a reckoning," said the butler; " would it might choke them!"

'Amen !" said every one.

" And master preacher there read me a lecture, and said a grace of a good ten minutes' length, and then fell to at trencher and wine-cup, like a crop-eared varlet as he is," said the house-steward, "and complained of the claret being over thin, d—n him!"

" Amen," said the butler.

" I will away," said Janet, " for fear of discovery, for I would not be taken and shut up before I give

Master Bachell warning of what guests he hath within."

So saying she alighted safely on her feet, and sought by the same hidden track her station behind the walnut tree. She had not remained long, before she saw shadows of the whole company standing up at the raised table, and heard a muttering sound which she doubted not arose from Master Browne saying grace after meat. This lasted some five minutes, and shortly afterwards the horses were brought round, and the company mounted and rode past her, with Master Pym at their head, and the preacher and Roger Priver closing the rear.

Janet, as soon as they were out of hearing, ran down to the Lodge-gate, and found that her father had been released, with strict orders to inform four troopers who had been left within when Master Bachell or his son Julian should arrive.

" I will see them all on the top of Dunkery hill first," said the gate-keeper.

" Or rather at the bottom of its iron mines, father," said Janet, " as being nearer to the place best suited to their puritanical persons."

CHAPTER IX.

MERRY were the crew of the lugger as she sailed
before a slight but favouring breeze towards her
haven, for they knew nothing of what had occurred
since their leaving Culbone Cove. All sat smoking,
singing, and talking by turns, and expecting to meet
their friends at Minehead. Master Giles Tudball
was in the bows conning, and Will Bowering at the
tiller, steering and telling marvellous lies at intervals,
to the amusement of Hugh de Mohun, the quack-
salver, and his man Jansen.

" Come, Master Giles, yonder lights show us the
quay of Minehead ; we have rounded Greenaleigh
Point, and, but that the flat shore forces us to keep
rather far out, a short half-hour would see our
warps made fast to the pier," said Hugh.

"We had been there long since, had there been more of a wind," said Giles. " I doubt not but that Master Richard and his wife will have brought themselves to an anchor in their own tap-room ere this, for they have but half our distance to go, and their galloway is fleet."

" Yon lazy lubber at the tiller hath not whistled once for a wind," said Hugh, "for, what with telling lies and puffing forth smoke, his mouth hath had no holiday."

" Foul fall the tale-teller, he was afraid to whistle, Master Hugh, lest his false breath should rouse the grey woman of Minyead," said Dr. Graveboys.

" Keep thee to thy pills and thy unguents, Master Doctor," replied Will, " I fear Mistress Leckey's wraith less than thou dost the ghosts of those whom thy filthy drugs have laid low in the churchyard."

" Nay then, if that be so, shew thy bravery and whistle now," said the doctor, " louder—louder still, for she may be at Waterford or Lundy Island and can scarce hear so coward a sound, at so great a distance."

Will, being so near to port, and in company, complied, and sent forth a clear, loud whistle, but the sound had scarcely died away, when a loud flapping as of wings was heard, and the light of Will's pipe, which he had resumed, shewed his face turning ghastly pale.

" D—n—I mean Lord preserve us ! it is the grey woman," cried Will.

" Tush man, be not fool and coward to boot," cried his master ; " it was but a sea-mew, whom your silly whistle convinced that we had another gull, and that is yourself, on board."

" Never mind," said Hugh, " It will make a proper subject for a new lie when you get on shore ; you can swear that you heard her speak in a loud clear tone."

" What ho ! lugger ahoy !" shouted a loud deep-toned voice, just as Hugh had done speaking.

" Lord help us !" cried Will, " see what it is to jest with the dead."

" Lugger ahoy ! lay to," said the same voice.

" Heaven help us, for nought else can," groaned Will.

"Peace, fool, and down with the helm hard. It is the voice of honest Robert Quirke, and yonder is his boat just ahead of us," said Giles, "what ho! what cheer, messmate?"

"Hold on by the painter, while I step aboard," said Master Quirke, laying his skiff alongside and shipping his sculls. "Now make her fast to the starn, and up with your tiller into mid-channel: Minyead must not see her Blossom in harbour to-night."

"How so? hath the gauger informed against us?" said Giles.

"The gauger hath not uttered a word that the customs officers might not hear and smile at," said Robert Quirke "but there be those at Dunster, that might seek at Minyead certain revellers and such-like, who have set at nought the orders of the parliament, and maltreated its officer in the lanky person of Master Roger Priver."

"And how knowest thou these news?" inquired Hugh de Mohun.

"The warder of the gate wherein Master Snelling liveth brought them to me at Minyead; he came thither to warn the pupil that the tutor was a prisoner on his account."

" And what more said Basil Chipera? said he that Master Thomas Luttrell was returned?" asked Hugh.

" He hath not returned, but is expected home this night.   Master Pym hath taken possession of the Castle, under the pretence of asking hospitality for himself and his troopers ; and Mistress Luttrell does not dare to say him nay."

" What is your advice in this strait ?"

" That you go forward with me to the mouth of the Hone, the Dunster river, where, as you know, I have a store-house on the lower marsh: there I can stow you securely, and the lugger can find safe anchorage ; there also will the yatch of Master Luttrell cast anchor, and we can advise him of all that hath happened," said Robert Quirke.

" Thy plan is a good one," said Dr. Graveboys, " but as I fear neither Pym, parliament, nor prosecution, for my license authorizes me to sell my goods any and every where, I will to Minyead in Master Quirke's boat with my man Jansen, and thence to Dunster, whence I will bring such information to you all at Hone-mouth as may be of service, and no one a whit the wiser."

"A blast from my trumpet shall be a hint of friends nigh," said Jansen.

"Nay if thy tin lie on this, as it doth on other occasions, when it proclaims safety to the ailing, it were better it were silent," said Will Bowering.

"It will not turn a sea-mew into a dead woman, or the voice of Master Quirke into a wraith's shriek," said Jansen, as he followed his master over the lugger's side.

The doctor and his servant had not long quitted the vessel, ere another cry of "Lugger ahoy!" was heard.

"Who comes now?" said Hugh.

"Master Jenkins, as you may judge by his Welsh tongue," said Giles Tudball.

"Impossible!" said Hugh, "we left him behind us, and, as he has but a pair of sculls and a small square sail, it is not likely he can have come up with the swiftest boat in the Channel."

"Nay, you forget that she draws less water, and can creep close in shore, while we have been forced to keep a good offing, and that, with a wind astern, a square sail will carry such a cockle-shell as that before it, nine knots good."

" Who hath he on board with him ?" asked Robert Quirke, " for I see one in the stern-sheets."

" Master Richard Luckes or the bully butcher mayhap," said Giles.

" It is I—Julian Bachell; is Hugh de Mohun still on board ?"

Hugh stepped to the side, and in a few minutes shook hands with his friend as he leapt aboard. Julian as briefly as possible recounted to him all that had taken place since he quitted them. The boat of Master Jenkins was towed astern, and all the party agreed to go to the Hone's mouth and remain there until morning, as Master Jenkins did not fail to add to Julian's story an alarming account of the proceedings of Pym and his followers at Culbone.

The lugger's head was brought round and put up Channel. The wind began to increase so much, that before they reached the place of their destination it blew half a gale, and they were obliged to take in a double reef of all the sails. Will Bowering could not help asserting that they should have a storm for having insulted the grey-woman of Minyead, who was not to be summoned with impunity. The crew laughed at his fears—all but one, and that was Master Robert Quirke, who, as the reader knows, fancied he had sound reasons for dreading the old woman's powers. They arrived however, before the storm, which shortly followed, gained its height, and came to anchor in the Hone's mouth. After making everything snug on board, they reached the store-house, and found a comfortable shelter from the rain which began to fall heavily.

In the mean while, Dr. Graveboys and his man landed at Minehead, and having taken some refreshment at the Ship Aground, as an excuse for informing the harbour-master of the arrest of his son and Mistress Richard, left the quay, and went through the upper town and the little village of Alcombe to the town of Dunster.

The distance was about two miles and a half, and the doctor and Jansen were, from much practice, good and fast walkers; but, before they reached the base of Conygar hill, which impends over the town, the storm had commenced, and Jansen found his box of drugs a troublesome appendage to his shoulders.

"I would, master mine, that we had left this pack of thine at the Plume of Feathers in Minyead, for the wind acts upon it like the sails of the lugger, and I have already made three such lurches to leeward as well-nigh brought me up all standing in yon ditch," said Jansen.

"What! leave my medicaments, the tools of my trade, behind me? never! who knows but that they may have been at cut and thrust up at Dunster, and that my unguents and healing balsams may be in requisition; and, as for the wind it is behind us, and when we have rounded Conygar we shall be in shelter."

"Well, at any rate, it is better to be here on hard ground, than out in the Channel on such an evening," said Jansen. "Giles Tudball, I trust, is by this time in harbour."

"Ay, that he is; for, with such a merry breeze astern, his lively bark would not be long running into Blue Anchor Bay, especially as it is high tide, and he can keep close in shore. It is not a desirable night for Channel sailing truly, and yet one is there, with wind and tide against him, unless he be already arrived," said the doctor.

" And who may that be ?" asked Jansen.

" The good owner of yonder noble Castle, Master Luttrell, who was to sail from Clevedon this day with his fair ward : God preserve them both ! "

" Who is this fair ward, of whom men speak so praisingly ?"

" Mistress Prudence Everard, the orphan child of the last of the Everards of Luxborough, whom he left when on his death-bed to the care and protection of his oldest friend, Master Thomas Luttrell. She hath just completed her studies in some house near the College in Bristol, and was to give him the meeting at Clevedon this day, to be conveyed to Dunster Castle, which is henceforth to be her home."

The doctor was interrupted in his speech by a vivid flash of lightning, followed by a loud thunder-clap, and such a dash of rain as made both him and Jansen set off at the top of their speed, which they did not relax until they found shelter in the Luttrell Arms, the principal hostelry in the town.

Without stopping to dry his clothes. the doctor,

bidding Jansen remain within, sought the gateway of the Castle by the open road, but seeing,
by the gleam of a flash of lightning, one of the
troopers posted there as a sentry, he returned down
the road, and sought to approach the gateway by a
secret path that led round the foot of the hill
through bushes and briars.

Through this path the doctor with difficulty
found his way, and reached, by means of the ivy, the
window out of which Basil Chipera had made his
escape, and which belonged to the room occupied as
a sleeping apartment by Hugh de Mohun. At this
window, into which he was rather too stout to creep,
as it was barred, but not closely, the doctor shouted,
well knowing that the wind which was roaring
round the gateway would prevent the sentinel
hearing him on the further side. His shouts
soon brought to him Basil Chipera, who could only
tell him that Master Pym and his men were
in the Castle, and that the parson was with Mistress Luttrell, (considered as under arrest,) endeavouring to calm her apprehensions for her husband's safety. Master Roger Priver was also in

the Castle, reducing to writing the information he had furnished against Hugh de Mohun and Julian Bachell. Those who had been arrested were now confined in the keep. Master Robert Browne was acting as Prive rs amanuensis.

When he had acquired all the information he could from Basil Chpera, the doctor returned by the same path to the Luttrell Arms. He was now thoroughly soaked by the rain and the droppings from the shrubs and bushes; nevertheless, he announced to Jansen his intention of leaving him there, while he went down to the stores of Master Robert Quirke, to explain the state of things at Dunster Castle to those there assembled, and to ascertain whether the yacht, a little cutter of some thirty tons, had yet arrived.

"Not so, master mine;" said Jansen, "if you go, I go. Like master like man; or if you will stay here and dry your garments, I, who am parcel-dry, and somewhat cheered by a jack of ale, slightly spiced, will borrow a wrapper of good Dunster broad-cloth from mine host, and seek Master Quirke's store, and be back again speedily."

" Not so, good Jansen, I must e'en go, if it be but to retrieve mine honour, having pledged it to that effect."

" Then will I go with you, for it never shall be said, that a drop of rain and a gleam of lightning drove Jansen from his master's side. But you will take a cup of what our host holds better than all our specifies, a spiced cup of ale?"

The doctor consented, and, having finished the pottle, set out with his man, leaving his box of drugs in the care of the host.

The road to the marshes lay by the side of the river, which, though but a small stream at Dunster, grows gradually wider and deeper as it nears the Channel. It was famed in those days for its trout and salmon, which were taken in great numbers at certain seasons by means of stake or tide-nets. The ground on either side of it is wet and swampy, as it is liable to be flooded at every spring-tide. To enable persons to reach the mouth of it in safety, a sort of path, or *hard*, as it is termed, had been made of the shingles and rough stones obtained from Watchet.

Along this hard, the doctor and his man proceeded with very great difficulty, for, although the
moon was at the full, and it was not yet late, the
darkness was intense, and the rain drove heavily
in their faces; the wind too was still powerful,
and almost lifted them from their legs. They
pressed on however, having a glimpse of their road
from the frequent flashes of lightning, and, after
much exertion, reached the storehouse of Master
Quirke, and made their coming known by a blast
from Jansen's horn, though it could scarcely be
heard amidst the din of the thunder.

Within, they found very comfortable quarters, for
Master Quirke had lighted a large fire, and had set
out a substitute for a table, on which were heaped
such viands as Master Jenkins had been enabled to
rescue from the stores of Richard Luckes's booth.
and certain supplies of spirits which the world
said were always to be had in plenty in the storehouse, which was supposed to contain provisions and
other goods that formed the freights of its owner.

The party within were all very merry except Will
Bowering, who still believed that he had caused the

storm which was raging without, by exciting the wrath of the grey woman of Minehead. He was calming his fears as he best might, by copious libations, between which he muttered all the prayers he knew by heart, to deprecate the anger of the departed lady.

Doctor Graveboys and Jansen changed their wet suits for others furnished them by the owner of the stores, and then sat down and communicated to their friends all that they had heard at Dunster.

"I see nothing that need alarm us for those in the Castle," said Hugh de Mohun. "Master Pym, sour puritan though he be, will offer no insult, nor allow any to be offered, to Mistress Luttrell or Master Snelling. That crop-eared rogue, Roger Priver, may tell his lies an he list, and Master Browne write them down; but, if there be justice and justices in the land, we will defeat their measures."

"As to justice in these days," said Julian Bachell, "we must not expect it, for even King Charles, God bless him! cannot obtain it. I am the more alarmed however, for the safety of Master than for that of his lady."

"Fear not for him Master Bachell, he is used to the Channel, and, rely upon it, he hath, when he saw the storm brooding, run into Weston-upon-the-Sea, or into Watchet," said Giles Tudball.

"Hark!" cried Will Bowering as he sprang to his feet; "hark, I say—heard ye not a cry as of one in danger?"

All listened, but nothing was heard save the roar of the wind and the rumbling of the thunder.

"Will hath not got over his fears of the grey woman yet, though he be safe housed ashore," said Giles.

Will stood pale and trembling, and could not join in the laugh that was going round at his expense.

"I'll swear that I heard a cry," said he, "between the thunder-claps, and hark! by heavens! I hear it now; be it Mother Leckey, or the devil's dam, or the devil himself, I will see what it means."

Will rushed towards the door, but Jansen threw himself in his way, telling him not to make a laughing-stock of himself by his folly. Will however flung him aside, as if he had been a mere infant in

his powerful grasp, and threw open the door. All
the party sprung to their feet, for, amidst the noise
of the elements, the cries of human beings in distress
reached their ears.

"The squire of Dunster Castle!" cried Hugh de
Mohun; "it must be he, and in danger. Lanterns
Giles, lanterns, thou hast plenty at hand; I will
forth; and do you all follow, but Jansen, who shall
throw all this dry wood in a heap without, and set
light to it to serve as a beacon to show them friends
are nigh."

So saying, Hugh, followed by Julian, rushed
out, and a scene presented itself to their eyes,
which shewed that his conjectures had not been
unfounded.

CHAPTER X.

THE shore about Blue-Anchor Bay is very flat, and although, at high water, a vessel of much larger size than the cutter belonging to Dunster Castle could sail up the channel formed by the Hone with ease and in safety; yet the slightest deviation from the straight course, on entering the river's mouth, would be sure to be attended with disastrous consequences.

When Hugh de Mohun and his friends left the storehouse, they could distinctly hear cries for assistance, but so intense was the darkness that they could see nothing, until a vivid and prolonged flash of lightning shewed them a small vessel, cutter-rigged, lying on her side near the mouth of the river, about sixty yards below where they were standing.   The wind, which was blowing strongly up Channel, dashed the waves over her, and seemed at times completely to overwhelm her! the crew were in the rigging, and a second flash of lightning discovered to those on shore the figures of a man and woman standing on the after-deck, apparently lashed to the guy-rope.

" God help them!" cried Julian Bachell, " for the cutter will go to pieces before we can reach them."

" Not so," cried Giles, "she is on the sands and will hold together yet; now steady all, and listen to me. Master Jenkins, do you get your boat ready; Will, bring you a coil of rope, make fast one end to our warp, and put the coil in the boat. I and Master Jenkins, will pull off to the cutter, and when all are in the boat, a tug on the rope shall be your signal to haul us ashore."

" No small boat can live in such a sea as this I fear, and the tide is still running up," said Hugh.

" We will try however," said Giles, as he leapt into the boat with the Welshman; a few smart strokes of the sculls sent the little boat into mid-

stream, and they could at intervals see her struggling with the tide by the blaze of the signal fire,
which had been lighted by Jansen and was now
burning fiercely: when she had got about half
the distance from the shore to the cutter, a wave
took her, and she disappeared from view.

" I feared 'twould be so; the boat, our only hope
is gone down, and Giles Tudball—"

" Fear not for him or the Welshman, Master
Bachell, they swim like seabirds, and the tide will
soon bring them ashore; see yonder they are, struggling manfully toward us; heap up the fire Jansen,
for we must recover the boat when she drifts
ashore if we can see her," shouted Will.

As soon as he had seen Giles and Master Jenkins safely landed, Hugh de Mohun went into the
storehouse, and, aided by the doctor, ridded himself
of his boots and loose jacket and petticoat; he deposited his pistols on the table, and returned to
the party outside.

" Haul in the rope, Master Giles, and make one
end fast to me. I will swim on board the cutter, and,
by means of the rope, haul a hawser on board her,
and then escape is easy and certain."

"Nay, nay, Master Hugh, you go not to risk your life; the plan is a good one, and *I* will carry it out," said Giles.

"Fear not for me, Giles, thou knowest I can swim bravely," said Hugh, seizing the end of the rope, and looping it tightly over his shoulders : "I shall not take water here, but go down as far as the rope will let me, and so get the tide-stream in my favour—do you get ready to make fast the hawser, as soon as you see me on board."

Hugh ran down beside the stream for some hundred yards, which brought him opposite to the cutter, but a little below her. There he fearlessly plunged into the waves, and was seen buffeting them with his powerful arms. Julian and the Mediciner looked on in silence; Giles Tudball and the Welshman were busied preparing a strong cable-rope, which Will had got ready; and Jansen was busily employed feeding the fire with dry wood, which, being saturated with pitch and tar, burnt brightly in spite of the rain that continued to fall.

In a few minutes, which seemed hours to Julian and Graveboys, Hugh de Mohun was seen clinging to the cutter's man-rope; a loud shout proclaimed his success, and in another second he was on board her, and, with the crew, employed in hauling in the cable from the shore; a few minutes sufficed to make it fast.

"Bravely done and well!" said Giles Tudball, "had we but the boat now, Master Jenkins, all should be safe on shore in a few seconds: as it is we must trust to those on board to see to their safe passage."

"Look yonder," said Julian, " if my eyes deceive me not, we shall not risk the lives of Master Luttrell and his fair ward for the want of a boat."

" True enough; there floats my little skiff, keel upwards; a short swim shall soon enable me to renew my acquaintance with her," said Master Jenkins, as he waded out into the surf, and succeeded with little difficulty in drawing the boat towards the land, where, with the assistance of the others, she was drawn on shore, emptied of the water and launched again. The skulls could not be seen, but the owner and Giles Tudball drew her down to the spot where the hawser was made fast, and getting into her, made for the cutter by pulling hand over hand on the cable, which was drawn taught from the shore to the ship.

It was a work of some difficulty to gain the ship's side, as the waves ran so high, that the little boat was frequently nearly overset, and Giles and his companion, though holding on "like grim death," were nearly washed from their places by the surges that burst over them. Skilful and courageous, they held boldly on, and gained the cutter's side. Master Luttrell stepped in, assisted by Hugh de Mohun, and Prudence Everard, whom Hugh had fastened to his left arm by a handkerchief passed round her right wrist for fear of accident, timidly essayed to follow her guardian. Twice she made the attempt, but her courage failed her just as she touched the boat's side. Hugh placed his right hand round her waist, and sprung lightly into the skiff, but at that instant a mighty wave caused the boat to surge, and he and Prudence were thrown into the raging waters.

A shriek of agony passed the lips of Master Luttrell, and he would have sprung into the tide after his ward, had not Giles and Master Jenkins held him back, assuring him 'that he need fear nought, as the young de Mohun would safely convey his companion to shore.

These assurances seemed likely to be realized, for Hugh was holding his left hand aloft, with Prudence firmly bound to it, and breasting the waves, as he struggled manfully to land, with his right hand. Julian Bachell rushed into the stream as they neared the shore, and assisted them to land. The poor girl, who was half drowned by the water she had swallowed, and exhausted by the previons events of the evening, fell at Hugh's feet deprived of sense and motion.

He bade Julian unfasten the handkerchief that had bound them, and, when it was done, raised her in his arms and conveyed her carefully into the storehouse, where he laid her before the fire, chafed her cold hands, and poured a small portion of brandy into her mouth. Doctor Graveboys took a small phial from the pocket of his still dripping jerkin, and, applying it to her nostrils, in a few minutes she opened her eyes, and saw her guardian and all the party, including the crew of the cutter, standing gazing upon her. She cast a look of love upon her friend, of gratitude on her preserver, closed her eyes again, and burst out in a fit of hysterical crying."

Dr. Graveboys poured a few drops of the contents of his phial into a cup of water, and, stooping over her, contrived with Hugh's assistance to make her swallow a portion of it. It had a surprising effect, for in a few minutes the sobbing ceased, she opened her eyes again, and raised herself from Hugh's breast, on the which she had been reclining.

Master Luttrell lifted her from the ground and placed her on a seat, supporting her in his arms, and blessing God for having rescued her from a watery grave.

" And to you, my young friend, next to Him, are we indebted for our lives; trust me I shall never forget your conduct on this day. To you too, Giles Tudball and Master Jenkins, I stand deeply indebted, and will not forget to do my best to pay the debt. Master Julian Bachell, Prudence Everard thanks you for your aid; and Dr. Graveboys shall not want a friend henceforth, for the kindly part which he hath taken in restoring to me her who is to me as a daughter."

Hugh, Julian, and the rest, declared that all their exertions were repaid and their dangers compensated by the safety of Master Luttrell and his fair ward.

" Nor must I forget to thank Master Bowering and Jansen there, whose friendly beacon first gave us hopes of rescue, and enabled us to see the exertions which our friends were making for our safety."

Will made a low bow, and went out with Jansen to secure the boat. Hugh de Mohun inquired of the captain of the cutter how it was that he had contrived to get her aground.

" Why, you see, sir, when I saw the storm a-brewing, my advice was to run for Weston, and take shelter at Uphill; but Master Luttrell said me nay, and I was forced, against my will, to make the best of my way against a strong tide and a head-wind, which nearly drove us ashore on the Steep Holms. I kept on however, and, deceived by the light from the windows of this storehouse, which I mistook for the light on the pier at Minyead, whither I thought we were running, for I was confounded by the storm that raged, bump I came aground, and, but for your aid, might have passed the night in no pleasant situation, even if the cutter had not gone to pieces."

Master Luttrell, who had been leaning over Prudence Everard and anxiously inquiring into her feelings, finding that, beyond the excitement and the fears she had undergone, there was but little to dread, except the consequences that might follow from her being unable to exchange her dripping garments for dry ones, turned to Hugh de Mohun, and inquired of him the cause of their being at the storehouse.

Hugh de Mohun and Julian Bachell briefly recounted the events of the day, and Doctor Graveboys told him of the state of things at the Castle.

" Master Pym," said he, " is welcome to the use of my poor apartments, and to such hospitality as the Castle affords; for, though a fanatic and a disloyal person, he is still a gentleman; but Master Roger Priver and Master Browne, who have made enemies of friends, and sown dissension in

families where love only reigned before, shall troop
with the troopers, or my name be not Luttrell.
So, on for Dunster, for these dripping garments
will do no good to this maiden's delicate frame,
and Mistress Luttrell will be anxious and alarmed
for the safety of her eldest child, as she calls her. You,
Master Hugh de Mohun, may safely take up your
residence with me to-night, and invite your friend
Julian Bachell to do the same, for I will be bail
with Master John Pym for your appearing to account for your boyish frolics. You, Master Giles
Tudball and the rest of you, shall be under my protection at the Luttrell Arms in Dunster, where there
be loyal men enough to see that a king's justice be
not wronged by these new officers, unlawfully appointed by the parliament without the royal authority ;—so forward for Dunster."

Hugh, who had been employed in resuming his
large boots and the remainder of his dress, ventured to suggest that they should remain where
they were, until the storm was abated; but Master
Luttrell, deeming it better for Prudence and all of
them that they should brave the storm and so get

to the Castle, where they might retire to rest at
once, would not yield to his suggestions. Just
at that moment, too, Will Bowering came in and
said that the storm had suddenly ceased, and added
with an oath that he had heard a shrill voice in
angry tones cry out, "Saved! saved! saved!" which
he did not doubt proceeded from the grey woman of Minyead, who was incensed at having lost
her prey.   He called upon Jansen to confirm his
statement, but the Merry Andrew declared that all
he had heard was the cry of some waterfowl, as they
flew over to the neighbouring marshes for their
nightly shelter.   He added however, that the storm
had passed on to the eastward, and that the moon
was making her light visible.

The   fires   were carefully   extinguished,   and
Prudence, covered with a thick warm boat-cloak,
was conducted along the hard pathway supported
on one side by her guardian and on the other by
Hugh de Mohun, to whom she did not fail to pour
forth her thanks for his gallant conduct towards her.

" He hath acted a noble part, Prudence, and deserves our gratitude, which shall be shown in deeds

rather than words. You, who have talents in limning, shall paint a picture of your rescue, and I will take care that it shall be preserved as an heir-loom in my family; thus shall we immortalise the courage of Hugh and your talents in the art of painting, at the same time," said Master Luttrell.

"I fear me I shall not do justice to my subject," said Prudence, "for, with all a woman's fear, I closed my eyes that I might not see my danger, and heard only the assurances of my safety whispered by my preserver, amidst the roaring of the waves and the howling of the storm."

"Imagination will supply materials, and to-morrow, when all is calm, we will visit the scene of our disasters and see to the condition of our little bark," said Master Luttrell, as he hurried his ward with rapid steps towards the Castle.

Hugh de Mohun was too happy to talk; he felt that he had probably saved the life of the fair girl who leaned on his arm and of her guardian, for whom he had long entertained a high regard; nor was his happiness a little enhanced by the idea, that he should be enabled to form a more in-

timate acquaintance with Prudence, while the picture, which her guardian had suggested, was in progress.

These thoughts kept Hugh silent, and, as Prudence had enough to occupy her mind, and the Master of Dunster Castle was pondering on what had
taken place within his walls, no further conversation ensued until they reached the hostelry, a
small, long, low-fronted building called the Luttrell
Arms, which was situated near to the foot of the
steep road leading up to the gateway. There
they parted with Giles Tudball and the rest of
their friends, except Julian Bachell, who joined
them and proceeded with them to the Castle.

The gateway of Dunster Castle consisted of a
large square tower, battlemented and flanked by turrets at each corner. Its ponderous gates had not
been closed for years, as, during the peaceful reigns
of Elizabeth and the first James, nothing had occurred to render such a proceeding necessary: the
office of warder or porter was therefore almost a
sinecure, and the worthy little man, Basil Chipera,
who held the office, amused his leisure hours when

not engaged in his business, or in his duty as clerk of the parish, in gardening and in cultivating a fine lemon-tree, which grew against the south walls near the Castle-windows, and was the object of his constant care and regard.

The lower part contained two rooms, in which Basil Chipera lived and slept; above them were three other rooms, where Master Robert Snelling and his pupil had their habitation. They wanted no culinary offices, for they either took their meals in the hall, where the parson officiated as chaplain, or were supplied with what they required from the kitchen and buttery.

When Master Luttrell drew nigh to the tower, he was surprised to find the gates closed, and a sentinel, with his pike shouldered, marching up and down before them.

"What ho! sir trooper! are we living in warlike times, that my Castle is thus furnished, and closed against its rightful owner? Open, and let me pass."

" It is against my orders to let any one in without Master Pym's leave given," replied the man in a surly tone, and without stopping in his walk.

"Open to me sirrah, I am the master here; I am Thomas Luttrell."

"An thou wert the Speaker himself, with his Commons at his heels, I would not open to you without the orders of my commander, John Pym of Cutcombe," replied the man.

Hugh de Mohun dropped the arm that still rested on his, and, backed by Julian Bachell, stepped up to the trooper and bade him stand aside on peril of life, at the same time presenting at his head one of the pistols which he wore in his belt. Master Luttrell, however, bade him use no violence, but ring the large bell which was used as a summons to meals.

Julian obeyed, and rang a peal which quickly produced another trooper, who, upon hearing the names of those who demanded entrance, opened the wicket-door and admitted them; and, by the light of a torch which he carried, conducted them respectfully through the outer court to the ·inhabited part of the Castle.

CHAPTER XI.

MASTER Thomas Luttrell was ushered by the trooper into the hall of the Castle : Prudence Everard hung upon his arm, and Hugh de Mohun and Julian Bachell, followed in the rear. At the upper end of the hall, at the raised table where the family and their guests took their meals, while the inferior members of the household, the servants and retainers, sat at the tables below, was seated Master John Pym; by his side sat Master Robert Browne, busily employed in writing; and on the other side of him stood Roger Priver: the constables of Dunster, forming the bailiff's posse comitatus, were seated near the great fire-place, and with them some half-dozen soldiers.

The trooper, who had preceded the owner of the Castle, announced his presence, and Master Pym

rose from his seat, walked down the hall and greeted him stiffly and formally.   The blaze from the
huge fire threw a gleam upon the face of the parliament officer, and shewed it in all its disagreeable
sourness.   He removed his steeple-crowned hat
when he saw that a lady was leaning on Master
Luttrell's arm, and made a low obeisance, but without uttering a word.

I would beg you, Master Pym, as you have assumed the mastery here, to summon one of the
female domestics, that Mistress Prudence Everard,
who hath been exposed to the storm this night in a
way that may prove injurious to her delicate frame,
may speedily seek the repose she needeth, and be
placed under the protection of her who acteth to
her a mother's part."

" Master Luttrell, I war not with women, and
much less with Prudence Everard, the daughter of
my late near neighbour of Luxborough; that we
were not friends was not from any fault of mine, but
he was ever favourable to the party who would have
promoted the interests of Prelacy and Arminianism,
which I, in my conscience, have felt it my duty to

oppose. Mistress Everard, I pray thee to retire; I have business with Master Luttrell and these youths. Mauworth, conduct the lady to Mistress Luttrell."

The same trooper, who had ushered the party into the hall, took a light from one of the sconces, and, after Prudence had bidden good night to her friends, preceded her to the apartments occupied by Mistress Luttrell and Master Snelling, who received her with joy, and heard the account of her escape from danger with heartfelt 'gratitude. She then retired to rest, after partaking of a warm draught, which in those days was considered as a certain preventive of the ills ensuing from wetted garments and exposure to the night air.

But we must return to the hall.

" I marvel greatly, Master Pym," said the owner of Dunster Castle, " that, having taken possession, and I trust, been treated with all due hospitality, you should have deemed it necessary to place a guard at my gates, to make my servants prisoners, and to refuse admittance to myself and my friends."

" I regret that it has been my unpleasant duty
to act as I have done, Master Luttrell, but I act
upon due authority," said Pym.

" Have you the king's warrant for your acts ?"

" Tush, tush, Master Luttrell, I have the warrant
of those whose authority is superior to that of
Charles Stuart : the times are licentious, and require a stronger curb than he, who supports Laud,
him of Canterbury I mean, is likely to put upon
them. I have the Speaker's warrant to put an end to
revels, junketings and such like sports, which were
legalized by the father of your Charles Stuart, because they savoured of the holiday games encou-
raged in the times of prelacy and popery. I sent a
copy of the orders of the parliament to you,
amongst others, Master Luttrell, and I find that
one of your household, Master Hugh de Mohun
there, was amongst the first to promote the revels
and ale-drinkings at Culbone, to resist the authority of the parliament, and to maltreat and misuse
its subordinate officer, Master Roger Priver, whose
warrant to execute the office of high bailiff, of
which you unjustly deprived him, he hath torn into

shreds and trodden under foot. 'Shall I not visit for these things?'"

"Master Pym, I am a peaceable and a quiet man, and I will not argue with such as thou about the proceedings of those who, though the lowest estate of the realm, seem to me to wish to assume the entire power, and to put down the monarchy. I will only say, in my defence, that I received not a copy of the warrant to which you refer, for I was away late last evening to take charge of my ward at Clevedon, and, as thou knowest, am but now returned: in the next place, I deny that Hugh de Mohun—"

"The descendant doubtless of the Mohuns, who whilome held Dunster and many estates around it, and were zealous papists?" said Pym.

"I deny, I say, that Hugh de Mohun is one of my household: he sojourneth for a space with Master Robert Snelling, to be perfected in his humanities, before he goeth to Oxford to complete his education," said Master Luttrell, taking no notice of the interrogatory with which Pym had endeavoured to interrupt his statement.

" Master Robert Snelling forsooth! him whom men call the parson of Dunster?"

"Yea, and who hath driven me from my freehold, and from my flock, instigated thereto and supported by the Master of Dunster Castle, who calleth himself patron of the incumbency. How long, how long, O Lord?" shouted the deposed divine.

" Silence, good Master Browne, and let me hear what excuses the pupil of the malignant hath to offer," said Pym.

" I deny he truth of your assertions," said Hugh, " I went to the revels as to a mere holiday, and to keep my word with one who had challenged me to a trial of strength. I neither interfered with Roger Priver in the execution of his duty, nor did I destroy his warrant."

" He did both, and moreover did submerse me in the brook," cried the bailiff.

" Thou hast sworn to it," said Pym.

" He lies in his teeth," said Hugh, " I did all in my power to protect him and his followers there, as my friend Julian Bachell can testify."

" Master Julian Bachell will have employment

enough to defend himself," said Pym, "for Roger Priver hath put his hand to written testimony, wherein he asserts, and hath proved to demonstration, that
he aided and abetted thee in the riots at Culbone·
and his father, who will not deny that he received
my warrant and the proclamation, shall suffer the
penalties of his disobedience to the parliament."

"Punish me an you will, Master Pym, but
trust the word of one who never willingly spoke
an untruth—my father knew not of my going to
Culbone."

"It was by my fault and at my solicitations
that he went," said Hugh; "let the blame fall on
me. His father knew not of his going."

"Yet he read over to his father both the warrant and the proclamation before he went—I am
advised of that—and the old malignant, who boasts
himself on his loyalty, as he calls his prejudices
for Charles Stuart, went wide of home, lest he should
be called upon to suppress the devil's games."

"Master Pym," said Julian, "you are an old man
and I but a youth, or I would thrust your abuse
of my father down your throat with my staff here.'

" Nay, be not rash," said Master Luttrell, " Master
Pym cannot but speak in the language of his party,
which partaketh of the coarseness of the followers
by whom they are supported."

" Master Roger Priver, summon your constables,
and, in your office of high bailiff, take me into cus-
tody these hot-headed youths," said Pym.

"He is no longer high bailiff; as a magistrate,
armed with the king's authority, and lord of this
manor, I have deprived him of the office, for his
illegal support of yon deposed priest," said Master
Luttrell.

" Which the parliament, at my instigation, have
restored to him," said Pym.

"Let him shew his warrant of authority," said
Hugh de Mohun.

" Thou did'st tear it into shreds,"—said Roger
Priver.

" Thou liest, wool-comber," said Hugh.

" It was violently taken from me, and destroyed
by the flesh-seller, and thou, like to Saul of old,
did'st stand by and consentedst," said the bailiff.

Seize on them, Master Priver, and I will be
thy authority," said Pym.

Roger Priver took seven solemn steps towards the young men, and beckoned to his followers to support him. When he saw that they were drawn up in order behind him, he took another step in advance, and offered to seize Julian Bachell who stood nearest to him. Julian however, stepped back, and with the beating-pole, which he still carried in his character of an Exmoor forester, dealt the bailiff such a blow on the side of his head as laid him prostrate on the hall-floor.

"He hath resisted the parliament," cried Pym, drawing his rapier, "his blood be upon him."

Master Luttrell, though a peaceable man, drew in defence of his young friend, but, before he had crossed blades with Pym, Hugh de Mohun threw himself between them, and, drawing both his pistols, put one into the hands of Julian, and presented the other at the leader of the assailants. Pym dropped his point, and the constables, with the soldiers, who were merely militia-men and as yet unused to fighting, drew back while Master Priver scrambled up upon his legs.

"I warn thee, Master Luttrell," said Pym, "that

I act upon authority in arresting these youths, and, if any resistance be made, you will be held accountable."

" I am in my own house, Master Pym, and it never shall be said that, while I am owner of it, this Castle allowed its guests to be betrayed. You have taken possession, but shall not keep it, if my blade hold good—so stand aside, Hugh de Mohun, and let me not in ridding my Castle of an unwelcome intruder, and the country of a pestilent roundhead," cried Master Luttrell, as he thrust aside his young friend, and made a push at Pym.

" Use not the carnal weapon—use not the carnal weapon; but order the men of war to seize upon them," shouted Master Browne.

" Thou art right—I will not imbrue my hands with his blood. Mauworth bring up your men, and seize them all," said Pym.

" Hark, my men," said Hugh, "these pistols are but small, but they will do their duty—pause, and settle among yourselves which two of you shall fall, before you attempt to execute the orders of yon disloyal man."

The men fell back, and a pause took place. Pym,

Roger Priver, and the divine, consulted together, while Master Luttrell and the two young men re- treated backward, keeping a firm front to the enemy, until they reached the screen of dark-oak which ran across the hall near the entrance. Here they pla- ced their backs against the wainscot, and prepared to defend themselves against all attacks.

The conference between Pym and his allies last- ed for some few minutes: Pym then stepped for- ward and said, "A truce with this folly, Master Luttrell, we have odds in our favour. Lay down your arms, and throw yourself on our merciful con- sideration: leave those young men to the fate their folly deserves."

"Never, Master Pym; so do your worst," said Master Luttrell.

"Bailiff do your duty—constables and soldiers support the officer," cried Pym.

Roger Priver, who had resumed his pike and put on his skull-cap, brought his weapon to the charge and advanced upon the three, followed by his men and the soldiers. The click of the pistols was heard, as Julian and his friend brought them to the full cock, and blood would certainly have been shed

and lives lost, for Hugh never missed his mark, and
Julian was but little inferior to him in the use of
his weapon, had not the hall-door been flung open,
and Mistress Luttrell, accompanied by Master Robert Snelling, and followed by Basil Chipera and a
large body of the Castle servants, entered.

"How now?" shouted Pym. "Sergeant Mauworth, did'st thou not confine yonder men as thou
wast bidden?"

"I did as I was commanded, and secured them
all," said the sergeant.

"Ay, but though doors be locked and windows
barred, there be those that can find means of
escape," said Basil Chipera; "and, while Dunster
owns a smith and he can be smuggled into these
walls, its lawful servants are not to be kept in captivity while its master is being murdered."

"What means this usage, Master Pym?" said
Mistress Luttrell, advancing before the rest.

"It is the priest, mine enemy!" cried out Master Browne, as he saw Master Snelling come forward with the lady; "smite him hip and thigh."

"Silence preacher," said the lady, "I would

ask Master Pym why he, having received all due hospitality at our hands, repays it by threatening the lives and liberty of the owner of this Castle and his friends."

"Madam," said Pym, "I had nought against your husband; but Hugh de Mohun and Julian Bachell are proved on oath to have rendered themselves amenable to the laws, as has Master Luttrell, now that he hath aided in their rescue from those who have authority to arrest them."

"I deny that authority," said Master Luttrell.

"And I—and I too," added the young men.

"Master Pym," said Snelling, "you have, as I believe treated me in an unlawful manner, for which I might have my remedy hereafter; but I will forego all further thoughts of retaliation, if you will but listen to reason, and withdraw from the Castle with your forces."

"Hew him down!" shouted Master Browne.

"You see that the servants are armed," continued the parson, not heeding the preacher, "and fully equal to your force. The alarm hath been given in the town of Dunster, and ere many minutes elapse, the loyal people of the place will be within the gates, ready to defend one whom they justly love and esteem. I would save bloodshed, Master Pym; so, with the permission of the good Master Luttrell here, I beg you to vacate."

"Peace, surpliced knave!" said Pym, "and let me speak with your betters."

"Nay, I intreat you, use fair words, Master Pym; the priest acts on my authority," said Mistress Luttrell.

"I crave your pardon, lady; I knew it not," said Pym, sheathing his sword, and bidding his men ground their pikes, which Roger Priver was the last to obey. "I would speak with Master Luttrell."

"Say on then, but be concise, or I will not answer for the consequences, if the men of Dunster find you here, and know that you have threatened my life," said Thomas Luttrell.

"Wilt thou pledge me thine honor to appear before me when called upon, and to produce these two young men also?"

"I will, if thou wilt shew me an authority from King Charles, but not else. Your warrant being signed by the parliament only, I consider illegal, and will not obey it."

" Long live King Charles, and down with the parliament!" shouted the servants, headed by Basil Chipera.

" Circumstances are against me," said Pym, "but as sure as there is a power above the king's, thou shalt pay for this, Master Luttrell."

" Nay threaten not, but save thyself and thy men, while yet you may; stand aside there Basil Chipera, and let these men pass, take sufficient force with you, and see them safely outside the gates with their horses and arms, and then make all fast for the night. Master Pym, I bid thee farewell, and trust your next visit to Dunster Castle may be of such a nature as not to force me to be but a churl in my house. Master Priver, see that thou act not without better authority than that thou has acted on this day; and you, Master Robert Browne, practise more and preach less, lest your strange doctrines get you into further trouble. You, soldiers and constables, be peaceable and or-derly, and provoke not the townsmen, lest they give you a warmer reception than you calculate upon."

Master Pym made a low bow to the lady, put on his lofty hat, and passed out of the hall, followed by Roger Priver, who dashed his pike on the pavement with a loud "ahumph" of defiance, by the preacher, who looked at Snelling as he passed, and muttered something about "the abominations of the land;" and by the constables and troopers, who seemed very glad to have the opportunity of avoiding a struggle with the servants of the Castle.

Hugh de Mohun and Julian Bachell assisted Basil Chipera in clearing the Castle; and, when they had seen the gates securely fastened, sought refreshment and rest, which they greatly needed after all the events of a day so fruitful of incident and adventure.

CHAPTER XII.

WHEN Pym, followed by his troopers, mounted
like himself, and by Roger Priver and his men on
foot, left the gateway of Dunster Castle, and rode
slowly down the steep descent, everything in the
town below seemed quiet and tranquil. A light
gleamed here and there from a latticed window, and
a lamp, which indicated the hostelry, gave forth its
feeble rays, scarcely serving to shew the market-
house, a small octagonal building, open below its
slated roof, which stood exactly facing it. The hill
called Conygar, which impended over Dunster on
the opposite side to the Castle, looked like a huge
black mass from the thickly planted Scotch firs
which lined its sides.

"Where be these men of Belial, with whose loyalty

and zeal in the defence of their lord, Basil Chipera did threaten us?" asked Master Browne of Roger Priver, by whose side he marched.

" The muddlepates are doubtless sleeping off the effects of the ale they have absorbed since their return from the ungodly revellings, in drinking health to the King and confusion to the Parliament. They are wont to be more valiant over their cups than in the fray, and to shew their loyalty in words rather than in deeds. I would that my pike were better acquainted with their flesh than it is likely to be this night; but vengeance is mine, and I will repay the scurvy usage of this day at some future time; let them look to it," said Roger Priver.

" Silence, silence, there, bailiff! and you good master preacher, be silent," said Pym. " The law is powerful enough, in our hands, to compensate you for any ill-treatment you may have experienced in the execution of its orders."

" But I have been buffeted and well-nigh drowned, deprived of my warrant of authority, and made a mark for the finger of scorn to point at," said the wool-comber.

" Yea, he speaketh -but the truth, and I, a minister of the gospel, have been treated as the very scorn of men," added Browne.

" All which shall be set right in due season," said Pym; to which assurance the only reply was a deep groan from the offended dignitary and the preacher. The latter added his favourite cry under tribulation—" How Long? oh Lord! how long?" at which the constables and troopers uttered a nasal grunt by way of chorus.

" As I have been rudely thrust out of the Castle of yon malignant, Thomas Luttrell, and mean not to depart far hence until I have duly investigated the serious matters before me, concerning this day's rebellious acts, I shall put up for the night at the hostelry below, known by the name of the Luttrell Arms. So forward, good Mauworth, to see to our reception, and provide stabling and provender for our horses," said Pym.

" May it please you sir, I fear that our presence among men dedicated to the service of the owner of this castle and town may not be acceptable, and our reception not over-courteous," said Mauworth.

" It is a house of public entertainment, and I fear not any rudeness at the hands of its host or its guests, who know me as a neighbour and a justice ; ride on sir, and see all prepared for our comforts."

Manworth obeyed, and, striking his spurs into his horse's flanks, galloped down the hill into the town.

" Were I a justice of peace," said Roger Priver, "I would e'en take away the license to sell creature comforts from such hostels as the Luttrell Arms, where profane toasts and improper songs are nightly given and sung, as provocatives to deep drinking and abusive language ; it is a stumbling block and a stone of offence to such as be soberly inclined, to hear issuing from its doors and windows words of abuse directed against the godly of the land, and such as shew due respect to the parliament."

" I, even I," snuffled Master Robert Browne, " I, a preacher of the pure gospel, the resister of Laud's attempts to restore the papistical forms and observances, am nightly denounced in the common meeting room of yon hell-upon-earth, as no better than a Scottish calvinist—oh—oh! how long? how long?"

The troopers and constables uttered a chorus of "Oh! oh! how long? how long?" in which the wool-comber's voice predominated.

"Look for better times—look for a change," said Pym; "the nation is awakened from its sloth fulness; the plough is ready, the oxen harnessed, and it wants but the hand of one skilful in the art to guide the ploughshare. There will be stirring times ere long, and he that taketh not his station between the stilts, and doeth not his work without looking behind him, will be—but hark!—halt every one, and listen."

The soldiers stopped, as if suddenly changed to stone, at the word of their commander. Roger Priver and his men more slowly, but as quickly as they could, followed the example set them. The preacher asked the meaning of the sudden order to halt on their way, but Pym bade him hold his peace and listen.

"I hear nothing, Master Pym," said Roger Priver, after the party had halted for some five minutes, "but the wind rustling through the pine-groves on Conygar hill."

"Dost hear the sound of the hoofs of Mauworth's horse?" asked Pym.

"No truly, he has reached the inn, doubtless, and has already stabled his steed."

"I heard the tread of his horse distinctly as it entered the town; suddenly the sound ceased, and I fancied I heard a cry and a groan as of one unexpectedly assailed—forward, men, but be cautious. Constables be ready to support us."

So saying, Pym rode forward, but not at a rapid pace, followed by Roger Priver and his men at a sort of jog-trot speed.

They entered the narrow street of the town without meeting with any obstruction, and passed on towards the inn about a hundred yards. Master Pym, who was foremost, fancied he saw something lying on the road before him, and called a halt.

"Bailiff, to the front, and see what obstructs our way." Roger Priver marched forward. He had not gone more than twenty yards, when a struggle, a fall, and a stifled groan were heard, and the bailiff disappeared from the view of his friends.

"A snare, a snare!—the enemy—the enemy!" shouted Master Robert Browne; "he hath fallen into the hands of the Philistines."

"Charge! charge, and be steady!" cried Pym, as he set the example to his men by riding forward at a brisk trot.

"The rope, beware of the rope," was heard in the voice of Roger Priver; but, before the warning could reach the ears of those for whose benefit it was intended, Pym and his six troopers were thrown heavily to the ground; and, before they could rise, were seized by the hands of a multitude who seemed to spring from the ground.

"Long live King Charles and the noble Master Luttrell, and down with Pym and the Parliament!" cried one whose tones proclaimed him to be a Welshman.

"Out lanyards and make all taut," cried another.

"Ay, ay sir," said a third.

"Secure them, but offer no violence—I would not have a blow struck or a wound inflicted, though

I have unguents of no doubtful healing powers,"
said a fourth.

"Master mine," added a fifth, "do let us have
a little phlebotomy, an it were but to see if the
rogues' blood run red like honest men's."

"No jesting," said a sixth voice, "but hamstring
their horses, and bind their riders firmly."

"What means this violence?" said Pym. "I
command you in the name of the parl—"

Before he could complete his speech, a gag of
some kind was passed over his mouth, and his hands
were drawn closely behind his back. His girdle,
which held his pistols, and the band from which
his rapier hung suspended, were cut in twain, and
a groan from the horse, which had fallen with him
over a rope tightly strained across the street, told
him that the order to hamstring all the cattle was
being obeyed. Pym struggled hard to free himself, but the hands that held him were too powerful for him, strong as he was, to resist.

"Lie still, Master Pym," said a voice in his ear,
"and you will suffer no further injury—resist, and
this night may be your last: you have overacted

your part, and insulted and imprisoned men more beloved and respected than yourself."

Pym was forced to take this advice, for he was now on his back, with two powerful men holding him down.

A scuffle, and but a short one, took place among the constables. The sound of blows was heard, mingled with a few words, and those chiefly in the voice of the preacher Robert Browne, which was stayed evidently by something being tied over the aperture out of which the voice proceeded.

" Are all the horses disabled ?" asked some one.

"All; all as useless as a craft without a rudder," was the answer.

" Then bind the riders two and two, and away with them to the iron mines, where they may lie snug enough, without friend or foe finding their unworthy bodies."

"And what is to be done with these poor ham-strung beasts, whose groaning is almost like that of men ?" inquired another.

"Master mine, it strikes me that it were merciful to have them knocked on the head by our friends

here, and their carcasses thrown into the Hone,
the river which rises at Cutcombe where King
Pym, our prisoner, was born."

"Ay, ay, and let the stream carry them out to
sea, to the spot where Master Luttrell well nigh
lost his life."

A groan or two, and a gurgling sound, as of blood
rushing forth, showed that the hint had been taken,
and a heavy tramp of men seemed to intimate that
numbers were not wanting to execute the orders for
conveying the horses' carcasses into the river.

Pym and his followers were placed on their
feet, and, supported by one on either side of them,
led forth, past the old priory of Dunster and its ancient church, leaving the market-place and the hostel on their right hand. The march was performed
in silence, and they quitted the town without so
much as a single light being shown by which they
might see the figures and faces of their foes; the
moon too had long withdrawn her light.

We must leave them on their march towards Dunkery hill, at the foot of which were the iron mines,
in which it was evidently the intention to imprison

them, and return to Ashley Combe Lodge, the seat of Master Bachell, Julian's father, which, the reader will be good enough to remember, was left in the possession of some of the troopers of Master Pym.

Janet, the gate-keeper's daughter, did not for one moment relax from her vigilance, in order that she might apprise her master of the unwelcome result of his son's having accompanied his friend, Hugh de Mohun, to the revels at Culbone. Her father's commands to quit the road and go to bed, though often repeated were not obeyed; she was resolved to await Master Bachell's return, let the consequences to herself be what they might.

Though the young May moon went down and left her in comparative darkness, still she walked slowly backwards and forwards between the little hamlet of Porlock-wear and the lodge in which her father dwelt, and listened anxiously for the footsteps of the horses, which bore her master and his attendant. At length, as the clock of Dunster church sent its booming notes over hill and vale, proclaiming the hour of ten, she distinctly heard the tread of horses, and rushed down a narrow pathway through the woods, which would enable her to stop the riders at a wicket-gate, through which they must pass to enter the bridle-track that led to Ashley Combe.

Master Bachell was surprised when Janet seized his bridle, and begged him to stay and listen to what she had to tell him before he approached his house; and Alick Pearson, his groom, was not a little alarmed, that she, to whom he had plighted his honest troth, should be wandering about in the gloomy woods of Ashley Combe at so late an hour. The surprise of the master, and the jealousy of the groom, however, were allayed when they heard all that Janet had to impart. Her master bade her return to her home and retire to bed, but to be stirring in the morning, and give the servants notice that he knew of all that was going on, and to bid them offer no resistance or insult to the troopers left in possession of the Lodge.

Alick, stooping from his horse, kissed her cheek, and told her to take care of herself, and not let any of the rude soldiers see her, for fear her beauty should overcome their puritanical morality.

Janet smiled as she tripped off to the Lodge, and Master Bachell, turning his horse's head, rode at a smart canter, followed by his groom, through Porlock-wear and Porlock village towards Dunster, intending to ascertain the fate of his son and his companion, and to offer what assistance he might to Mistress Luttrell, in case her husband should not have returned from Clevedon.

Just as he arrived at the spot where the road branched off, on the left by Minehead to Dunster, and on the right by the base of Dunkery hill to the upper part of the town and the keep of the Castle, his progress was arrested by a procession which occupied the whole of the narrow road.

"Alick, come up and keep at my side; prepare your pistols, but do not fire unless we are attacked. This may be Master Pym and his party on their return, or it may be merely Giles Tudball and his sumpter horses, or his sumpter men trafficking inland: at all events be prepared and do as I do."

Alick rode up to his master's side, and drew a huge pistol from its holster, and, in his eagerness to ascertain whether friend or foe was before him, called out " Who goes there ?"

" Who asks the question ?" said some one springing from under the shade of the nut-tree hedge,
and seizing his bridle.

" It is I—Bachell of Ashley Combe."

"Then, good sir, you are among friends—ride on
to Dunster, where you will find your son in safety
with the lord of the Castle. You will easily
obtain admittance, for we have the gentlemen who
were rude enough to take possession of it in our
safe keeping, and mean to let them pass a quiet
night in one of the mines here in Dunkery hill."

" I should know that voice," said Master Bachell, "and if I err not it belongs to Dr.—"

"Hush, good sir, hush !" said the mediciner "the
locks about the ears of Pym and his puritans be so
closely clipped, that not a whisper escapes them."

" Whom have you, with you then ?" asked Master
Bachell whispering.

"I will just give some orders to my man Jansen,
and be with your worship anon," said Graveboys.

In a few seconds, the master of Ashley Combe
could see the body of men who had halted at his
approach pass through a field-gate on the right
of the road, and enter upon a path which he knew

led across an open wild common to the entrance of the iron mines.

Graveboys returned as soon as the whole of the body of men had passed on their way, and explained to Master Bachell, as briefly as he could, all that had happened during this memorable day; and how that he, Giles Tudball, Master Robert Quirke, Jenkins and others, assisted by the loyal people of Dunster, had seized and gagged Master Pym and his followers, and were going to confine them in the iron mines, until Master Luttrell, Hugh de Mohun, and Julian Bachell, should have taken what measures they deemed necessary for their present safety.

Master Bachell seemed to think that the cousequences of their rashness would be serious; but the mediciner assured him that they had taken such precautions, that none of the party who had executed the bold seizure of Pym, his troopers and followers, could ever be known. He begged that no violence might be offered to any one, and having obtained a promise to that effect from Graveboys, who assured him that every one should be released as soon as Master Luttrell's pleasure should be known, he rode off to Dunster with Alick, as fast as his horse could carry him. He avoided the town, and gained the gates without meeting a soul. Basil Chipera, who was keeping watch within, after having seen Pym's troop-horses committed to the stream of the Hone, gladly admitted him within the walls, and obtained for him and his servant, lodgings in the Castle, although its owner and the family had retired for rest an hour or two previously to his arrival.

Basil Chipera took the horses to the stables, and having supplied them with provender for the night, left them, with the promise of a good grooming in the morning, and sought his own chamber in the lower room of the gateway of Dunster Castle, but not before he had seen the gates securely fastened.

CHAPTER XIII.

WHEN Pym and his party were safely thrust into the iron mines, at the foot of Dunkery hill, and their escape prevented, by heaping up large stones at the entrance, Master Robert Quirke, who, at the instigation of Basil Chipera, had been the principal actor in the attack, called his party together, and made each individual take a most solemn oath, never to divulge the names of any one who had had a share in the illegal proceeding.

He found no one unwilling to take the oath required of him, as none but those who were well-affected towards the owner of Dunster, and, what was beginning to be called, the king's party, were allowed to join in the attack.

Quirke and Graveboys, when they agreed to con-

fine Pym, and so allow Master Luttrell time to decide upon his plans, had both of them stipulated,
that no violence should be offered to any one, beyond what was absolutely necessary for securing
their persons, and preventing them from alarming
the town by cries for help.   In this they were
ably seconded by Giles Tudball and the other principal actors, who had no ill-will against any one,
except perhaps, Roger Priver, and Robert Browne
the preacher; and their ill-feeling towards them was
not sufficiently strong, to urge them to offer them
any serious violence.   The mines, in which it had
been agreed upon to imprison them, were neither
deep nor dangerous ; they were on a level with
the valley, and well ventilated by fissures in the hill
above. Robert Quirke, too, before he left the mines,
and he was the last to do so, took care to free Master Pym of the belt which bound his arms, and the
strap that gagged his mouth, so that he might be
at liberty to set all the rest of the prisoners free.
He also, wisely took the precaution to disarm all
the party, in case, which was not unlikely, they
should quarrel with each other during their con-

finement; for, although they had acted together in their attacks on the revellers and the malignants, as they called the Bachells and the Luttrells, the constables and troopers were not as yet prepared to go the lengths to which Pym, the Preacher, and Roger Priver would have urged them.

They were opposed to popery and prelacy, but had not yet forgotten the feelings, of loyalty and respect for the gentry around them, in which they had been brought up. Mauworth, who was a tenant on Pym's estate, and treated by him as a confidential person, would have sided with his landlord in case of an open rupture; but he had been heard to say, that he thought Master Pym was going a little too far and too fast.

When the Dunster men had taken the oath imposed upon them by Quirke, they hastened back as rapidly as they could to the town, and sought their beds. Dr. Graveboys and Jansen went with the host of the Luttrell Arms, and put up at his house for the night—or rather morning: Robert Quirke returned to Minehead, with Tudball and Will Bowering; while Master Jenkins sought

the stores on the banks of the Hone where he had
left his boat, in which he meant to reach the Blossom of Minehead, and sleep on board that lugger.
The whole party effected their objects so successfully, that no one was aware of their having been
absent on so desperate a business, but those who
were not likely to betray them.

Before they parted, it had been settled that
Dr. Graveboys should see Basil Chipera early
on the following morning, and learn through him
the wishes of Master Luttrell, concerning the dis-
posal of Pym and his party, and if any danger was
likely to result from their imprisonment, that the
principal actors in it, should get out of the way until
the danger was over. The arms, which had been
taken away from the prisoners, were hidden in a
brake, hard by the mouth of the mines.

The first act of Pym when he found himself at
liberty to speak, was to address the soldiers and
constables, and bid them submit quietly to the
fate that had befallen them : his second was to release Mauworth and the preacher from their bonds,
and to assist them in releasing the others. The

moment Master Robert Browne found his tongue at liberty, he burst out with his usual "how long? how long?" which produced a deep groan from every one but Roger Priver, who, forgetting the presence of Master Pym, no sooner found the gag removed from his mouth, than he uttered an oath against the men who had bound him, of so frightful a nature, as caused him to be severely reprimanded.

"Hath no one a light, that we may see the nature of the place, in which our enemies have confined us?" inquired Pym.

Some half-dozen men produced flints, and struck a light with their knives, catching the sparks in some tinder which they carried with them for the purpose of igniting their pipes. Mauworth produced some matches which he had about him, and succeeded in lighting one of them. By its short and flickering rays, they could see that they were in a sort of cavern, from which passages branched in all directions: they had not time to examine either of them, for before the light of the match had been exposed one minute, a flutter of wings was heard, and the match was extinguished by something that flew against it. Another was ignited, which speedily shared the fate of its predecessor; and so alarmed the whole party, that they believed the preacher's assertion that Beelzebub was among them, and begged of Mauworth not to persevere in his attempts to enlighten those, who were evidently for a time, under the power of Satan.

"They be but bat-mice," said Roger Priver, "and were they devils I will have a light. I cannot endure this darkness."

He seized a match from Mauworth, and kindled a flame from his tinder; it flickered brightly for a moment, and was suddenly extinguished by something that struck him at the same time so sharp a blow on the face, as brought the tears to his eyes, and caused a small stream of blood to trickle down his cheek.

" May the curse of—" commenced Roger Priver.

" Swear not at all," said Pym, " the attempt to gain a light is useless; let each man betake himself to sleep, and see what the morning will bring forth. Mauworth, I would speak with you apart."

The sergeant, following the direction of his commander's voice, succeeded in reaching him; and Pym, taking his hand, led him up the cavern, until he had reached such a distance from the rest, as he thought would prevent the tenor of his words being heard.

"Mauworth, I have no reason to doubt your fidelity," said Pym, "but I cannot account for your allowing us to fall into an ambuscade, without giving an alarm."

"An it please you, sir, my horse stumbled over a rope, or some other obstruction, placed across the street of Dunster, and threw me over his head. I essayed to shout to give you warning, but ere a cry left my lips, my mouth was gagged, and I was held in the grasp of many men, against whose strength my struggles were unavailing."

"I guessed as much," said Pym in a whisper; "but tell me sergeant, if you can, who were the leaders in this base attack on the authorities appointed by the parliament."

"I know them not," replied Mauworth, "so that I could positively swear to them, for they

spoke not a word that I could hear distinctly ·
but I have my suspicions."

" And on whom do they fall?" asked Pym.

Mauworth was about to name some of the parties concerned, when he was interrupted by a hub-
bub from the farther end of the cavern, caused by
the high bailiff, and the troopers and constables, mutually accusing each other of being the
cause of their being shut up in a loathsome prison,
for a long night.

" We must quiet them, sir," said Mauworth
"or they will get to blows."

"Peace, peace ; " shouted Pym, "and do you
Master Browne offer up a prayer, and then let all
seek the repose we so much need."

The preacher needed no further orders, but at once
commenced a prayer, which, as it was an impre-
cation of everything undesirable upon the head of
his enemies, might have been safely called a malediction.   The commencement of it acted as a sti-
mulaut on his hearers, and was received with many
marks of approbation; but when he left off abusing
the men of Dunster, the malignants of the Castle,

and of Ashley-Combe, and the young men
who were educated in the unseemly schools
of papacy and prelatism; and launched out
into a rambling discourse on the titles and claims
he, as a servant of the gospel, had been unjustly
deprived of; his words operated as a sedative and
lulled most of his hearers to sleep. He was
not aware of this effect, until in the midst of a severe censure upon Master Snelling, who had thrust
him from his rightful pulpit, Roger Priver uttered
so loud, and so prolonged a snore, as awakened an
echo throughout the mines.

Master Browne was indignant; he raised his
foot, and· guessing from the sound, whereabouts
Roger was lying, kicked him as `hard as he could:
the kick only produced a louder snore, and the
preacher after inquiring "who hath ears to hear?"
without receiving any answer, seated himself with
his back against the sides of the cavern, and speedily
followed the example set him by his congrega-
tion. They slept soundly for some time, for they
were wearied by the long day's toil, and by their
march from Dunster; but were aroused by a sud-

den, sharp cry, which caused them all to spring from their places, and seek the arms which had been taken from them.

"Blood, blood, more blood—ahah!—Say not *I* did it—you had a fair trial—a jury of your peers found you guilty—ahah! the laws—the laws—blame *them*—blame not *me*. Avaunt, thou headless thing."

The cavern rang with the cry, and every man's heart palpitated as he heard it.

"What means it?" said Roger Priver in a whisper heard by all.

"What means it?" said a voice which they then knew to be Master Pym's. "What means it? ye false friends—ye base churls—to suffer the guilty Strafford to thrust his headless trunk into my presence, and accuse me of his murder—what ho! Mauworth—take me hence—I will stay here no longer; remove *him* or carry me hence—I am choking."

"God's judgment," said one of the Dunster constables, to which a deep groan was responded.

"Hush, my friends, hush! he sleeps, and

dreams as he sleeps; I will awaken him," said Mauworth.

The men huddled together and trembled, as they held each other's hands, to hear the frightful shrieks that issued from Pym's lips, until his sergeant had succeeded in rousing him to a state of consciousness. When he was fully awakened, and apprized of what he had uttered, he excused himself, by saying that he had had a frightful dream, and begged of them to seek repose again.

They were all of them however, too much alarmed to sleep, and huddled together, as patiently as they could, waited until morning should dawn upon them. They did not dare to make any audible remarks on what had alarmed them, for fear they should reach the ears of Master Pym, who was now conversing with Mauworth as rationally and calmly, as if nothing had occurred to disturb him.

Master John Pym, although he had from the commencement of his parliamentary career, universally opposed the royalists, and taken an active part with Mr. Hampden and those who resisted the payment of the ship-tax, was gentlemanly in his demeanor, and mild in his manners and language, until he had rendered himself so obnoxious to the king, that he came into the house, shortly after the assassination of Buckingham, to seize him and four other members. Pym escaped the danger, and absented himself from the house for awhile. When he returned, a change was observed in him: he was more severe in his looks, and his language was violent : he took the lead of his party, and when the impeachment of the Lord Strafford was determined upon, he untiringly persevered in his attempts to secure his condemnation and execution. He was also the bitterest enemy of the established church, and lost no opportunity of assailing the bishops, and the deans and chapters; and of encouraging those, who, under the pretence of their being remnants of papistry, sought to remove the communion tables and the rails which surrounded them, from the eastern ends of the churches. Nothing in fact, was proposed to injure the church, in which he was not a prominent actor. Of all the enemies whom Archbishop Laud had, none was more perseveringly bitter than John Pym, although they were contemporaries at Oxford; Laud being a member and president of St. John's college, and Pym a student of Broadgates Hall, now Pembroke college.

As a country gentleman, Pym was much beloved; he was a kind husband, an affectionate father, and a considerate landlord to his tenantry. As a neighbour, his company was sought after and appreciated by those, even, who differed from him in politics, until after the execution of Strafford, when he suddenly found himself shunned by all who had previously courted his society.

He grew morose and peevish; seldom appeared in Somersetshire, and made the leadership of his party in the commons, an excuse for absenting himself from his family. His moroseness increased, too, greatly, after his intercourse with the Scottish Covenanters, who were referred to him as the most powerful person upon whom they could rely to advocate their claims.

It was in the midst of his conferences with these opponents of a ritual, that he had been summoned into Somersetshire, by news of the illness of his wife, and while watching over her during her convalesence, he had heard of the intended revellings at Culbone, and taken the proceedings which led to his temporary confinement in the mines of Dunkery hill.

" Mauworth," said Pym, "tell me, and tell me truly, what I have said that those fools yonder are alarmed at."

Mauworth repeated to him the words he had uttered in his dream.

" Will it ever be thus? will the vision never leave me? I would that daylight were come, for the gloom and heavy air of this cavern oppresses me.   What hour is it, think you?"

" Nay, sir, I know not, and I fear me that unless those same caitiffs, who have entombed us, remove the obstacles at the mouth of this cavern, we shall be long ere we discern day from night," said Mauworth.

" They cannot mean to murder us: to leave us here to die of famine," said Pym, " Would to God we had resisted, and been slain in fair fight, rather than die and rot here."

"We can at least make a struggle for our liberty: we are a strong body, and may force the entrance, which they can have barred only with loose stones and rubbish," said the sergeant.

"Let the trial be made instantly," said Pym, "for I feel as if I should be suffocated."

The bailiff and his men, and the troopers, were ordered to set about trying to remove the obstacles that closed the entrance They worked long and resolutely, but having no instruments to assist them in their task, made but a slight impression on the bulk of stones that had been heaped at the mouth of the mine.

When they were exhausted with their attempts, and had given them up in despair, they threw themselves upon the ground, firmly persuaded, that the cavern in which they were confined would be their burial place. Robert Browne, in his alarm, commenced chaunting the burial service of the church, aided by Roger Priver; and Pym, with his sergeant at his side, paced up and down the mine without speaking a word.

Suddenly a noise was heard at the entrance,

like the fall of masonry, which grew louder and
louder.   All sprung to their feet, and their hearts
leapt in their bosoms when the light of day shone
in upon them; and then each man rushed to
the opening, and assisted those without in removing the rocks which still opposed their escape.
When an opening wide enough to admit the passage of a man was made, Pym stepped forth, and
saw Master Luttrell and Master Bachell, with a
strong party of Dunster men waiting to receive
him.

CHAPTER XIV.

WHEN Master Pym stepped forth, followed **by** his party, neither of the gentlemen who had come to release them, could refrain from laughing. The soil of the mines, a kind of red ochre, had stained their clothes and persons, so that they looked like a body of wild Indians rather than Englishmen. The Dunster men, when they beheld Roger Pri-ver and their other towns-fellows, the constables, so strangely disfigured, fairly shouted with glee, and were so boisterous in their laughter, that Master Luttrell was compelled to threaten them with his severest displeasure, if they did not cease their unseasonable clamour.

When silence was somewhat restored, Master Luttrell addressed Pym, and told him, that he deeply

regretted the unworthy manner in which he had
been treated, and that the moment he was informed by Master Bachell of what had occurred,
he had summoned his retainers and hastened over
to release him.   He added that he would use his
best exertions to discover, and punish the parties
who had been guilty of so gross an outrage.

"He lieth, he lieth! believe him not; it was
the malignant himself that gave the orders to
his ungodly dependants to confine us, while he and
yon other malignant there, might lay their plans,
to ensure the escape of those who disobeyed the
warrant of Master Speaker, and the parliament,
and insulted their officers—"

"Aye, and did plunge them in a brook, and
tore up my warrant of authority—oh! oh!"

"Silence, good Master Browne; be silent,
Bailiff of Dunster; your wrongers shall not go unpunished: the proceedings of yesterday and the
past night shall be laid before the house of commons: let Master Luttrell and Master Bachell
look to it: Dunster Castle and Ashley-Combe
Lodge may find other owners shortly, in men

more inclined to be obedient to those, to whose hands the people have entrusted the supreme authority," said Pym.

" While we have a king and a house of peers," said Master Bachell, " I for one, shall not acknowledge the supremacy of the lower house; more especially when it is made up of violent men, who curry favour of the lowest of the people, and seek to gain an ascendancy in the state, by pandering to their basest passions."

" Nor I," said Master Luttrell. " I am a magistrate as well as yourself, Master Pym, and as zealous in the due administration of the laws ; but I cannot esteem any warrant legal, that has not the authority of the king—God bless him."

Master Luttrell raised his plumed hat from his brow, and his example was followed by all his party, who uttered a loud shout of "Long live King Charles."

" How long ?—how long ?" groaned the preacher.

" Heed them not, Master Browne," said Pym, "let them shout their loudest. It may gratify them to cry, 'Long live the king,' but let them shout as loudly as they will, Charles Stuart must have good ears to hear them, seeing that he is sojourning in York."

While Pym addressed these few words to the preacher, the leaders of the Dunster party, were begging of their followers not to indulge in any remarks, or utter any shouts which might be reported to their disadvantage. They ceased shouting therefore, but turned such threatening looks on their opponents, as showed that they would gladly have used stronger language in their hearing, and even proceeded to blows, had the slightest hint been given to them by their superiors, that an attack upon the Roundheads would have been agreeable to them.

" May I ask, Master Pym, on what good grounds my poor house of Ashley-Combe, is invaded by your troopers or trained-bands as you call them, and my servants put under restraint ?" inquired Bachell.

" And I too would know, why I find, on my return from a distant voyage, my Castle converted into a prison, my wife alarmed, and the establishment thrown into disorder," said Master Luttrell.

"You shall both know, and that soon," said Pym, "that a strange thing hath been done in the land, and that too by your instrumentation. An offence has been committed against all godly men, and in direct opposition to the orders of the parliament. The young Hugh de Mohun, and Julian Bachell may generously, as youth is wont to do, take upon themselves all the responsibility of the unlawful doings at Culbone, but those who ought, by virtue of the authority reposed in them, to have prevented such scenes, shall not escape the punishment due to them, under the plea of absence from home, and ignorance of what was going on. For the unworthy treatment which I, and my followers here have experienced, in having been expelled by force from Dunster Castle in the night, and shut up in a close, loathsome cavern, I must have satisfaction—"

"Take it now," said Master Bachell, laying his hand on the hilt of his rapier.

"Nay, good Bachell," said Luttrell, "It was I who removed him from Dunster, of which he complains, and from me he shall have that satisfaction he requires. Draw, Master Pym fear not that you shall not have fair play, for I pledge you my word, that he, of my Dunster followers, who offers to interfere between us, shall have his ears cropped as closely as the hair of your retainers."

Pym smiled gloomily, as Mauworth and his followers drew up to his side, as if to support him, and said—" No, Masters of Dunster and Ashley-Combe; the insult has been passed upon the parliament through me its unworthy officer—"

"He never spoke a truer word; unworthy he is," said one of the Dunster men.

"And the parliament," continued Pym, not heeding the remark, "shall give me the satisfaction I require. I imbrue not my hands in the blood of my neighbours, in any private quarrel."

Mauworth looked disconcerted, and the preacher and Roger Priver groaned, as if disappointed at not seeing Pym fall on and slay one of the malignants, at least. Bachell and his friend exchanged smiles, accompanied by a curl of the lip and a shrug of the shoulders. The Dunster men laughed outright, and the words cowardly, crop-ear'd rogue, passed among them.

"You hear, good Master Pym—you hear," said Browne ; "let not our good cause suffer by witholding the strong arm. I myself, am ready for the fray, rather than our enemies should triumph over us ungodly. Smite them, even to the death."

"You forget we have no arms," said Mauworth.

"Be silent, I intreat you," said Pym, "no man who knows me, will accuse me of a want of courage ; a public offence hath been committed, and its punishment shall not be a private matter, but of such a nature, as to lead others to be unwilling to offend in the same way in future."

"We shall not shrink from any investigation legally made, into our conduct, and I pledge you my word as a gentleman, that neither my friend Bachell here, nor myself, will attempt to evade giving that satisfaction which the law can demand of us," said Master Luttrell.

"And the young men—Hugh de Mohun and Julian Bachell, they must be given up to us; they are our prisoners and—"

"Not so, you forget Master Pym, that you are

virtually our prisoners, seeing that we have you in our power, unarmed and unhorsed," said Master Bachell, "but I will be responsible for the appearance of my son, to answer any charge you may bring against him, in any lawfully constituted court."

"Our arms and our horses must be restored to us, and that instantly," said Pym.

"For your arms—search yonder bushes, and take them, and use them in a better cause than depriving the people of their innocent amusements, and alarming the servants and families of private gentlemen, when they are left unprotected; for your horses —if you would recover their bloated and swollen carcasses, go, follow the Hone to where its pure, fresh waters mingle with the salt waves of the Channel," said Master Luttrell.

"You have not dared to—"

"*I* have dared nothing," said Luttrell interrupting Pym, "I knew nothing whatever of the intended attack on your party after you quitted my Castle, neither did Master Bachell; but your conduct to two of your nearest neighbours and former friends, it seems, urged the townsmen of Dunster to resort to measures, that I would have prevented had I known of them in time."

Mauworth and Roger Priver had armed themselves and their men, as soon as the place where their weapons had been deposited had been made known to them, and before the short dialogue between Master Luttrell and their leader was ended, had formed themselves behind the latter. The Dunster men seeing their movements, drew themselves up behind their leaders, and by their looks betrayed their anxiety for a struggle to commence.

" Back, Mauworth—back, and draw off your men; heard you not that I said I would make of this grave matter no private quarrel?" said Pym.

"Ah Lord! and ah! his glory, it is departed," said the preacher.

" Oh—oh!" groaned Roger Priver, letting his pike fall heavily on the ground, an example which all the troopers followed.

" Men of Dunster, I will have no further violence committed," said Master Luttrell, " the evil that has been done already, may inconvenience you all more than you reckon upon; lay aside your arms."

" Nay, not so," said Master Bachell; " keep your arms in readiness, my friends, for, unless my eyes deceive me, yonder, along the road from Ashley-Combe, come some mounted troopers, who, by their dress and bearing, are a part and portion of Master Pym's trained-bands."

" Nay, there are but four of them," said Master Luttrell, "and we are a match for them at any rate."

All eyes were turned upon the four men, who, as soon as they arrived at the gate leading from the lane towards the mines, turned into it, and galloped up to their leader, Pym; each of them looked pale and haggard, and turned his head behind him as if he dreaded pursuit.

"How now, sirrahs?" said Pym, when he saw who the men were, "did I not leave you at Master Bachell's Lodge of Ashley-Combe, and bid you remain there until further orders? what has driven you thence thus hastily, and with the marks of cravens on your brows?"

" The devil'" said the foremost of them.

"Sathanas, Sathanas!" said the rest, groaning, in which they were aided and assisted by Robert Browne, Roger Priver, and the troopers.

"Cease your clamour and tell me plainly, what means this nonsense?" asked Pym.

" The devil—the devil—sathanas—sathanas! " groaned out the four together.

" They have been over-free of the wine-pot, and are now but parcel-sober," said Mauworth.

" Good comrade Mauworth, and you most honored sir, we are most sober, seeing that the churl of a butler at Ashley-Combe, would supply us with nothing but fair water from the spring, after your departure, saying that even that was too good for such as we."

" He showed his prudence if not his hospitality," said Pym; "but what happened to you to alarm you ?"

"The dev—"

" Pshaw! man, facts," said Mauworth.

"Finding, honored sir, that no further bodily refreshments were forthcoming, and being somewhat fatigued with the exertions of the day, we

did lay ourselves down to rest, after locking up
the servants, and securing the outer doors, so that
no one could gain admittance without giving us due
notice, according to your honour's orders. The
beds truly were soft, and our slumbers were heavy,
yet did none of us rest long; for noises, such as
no earthly sounds resemble, disturbed us; and visitations from the fiends beset us at intervals, where-
of we bear the marks even now, as though we had
been cudgelled by mortal hands; and our couches
were moistened as we lay, either by the sweat
from our frightened bodies, or by water poured
upon us by the evil one."

"Oh! oh! how long? how long?" said Robert
Browne.

" Silence, preacher; and do you proceed, fellow,"
said Pym.

" We engaged in prayer, honored sir, and the
fiends left us awhile, but anon returned again, and
buffetted us sorely—"

"Fools!" said Mauworth, "did your courage
fail you, so that you could not discover your tormentors?"

" Our lights failed us, good Mauworth, and we were in the darkness of despair until day-light came, and shewed us everything as we had left it overnight : not a bolt or lock drawn or un-fastened; all the servants shut up in their respective rooms. One fair maiden from the gate-lodge, told us that the night had been fearfully stormy, and that she had seen lights and sights in the stables, such as had never been seen at Ashley-Combe be-fore, and truly when we sought our horses, we found them reeking with sweat, and covered with mud and foam, as though they had been ridden or driven all night long."

"Oh! oh! how long? how long? Satan hath pre-vailed," said the preacher.

" Well sirrah, and then ?" said Pym.

" And then," said the trooper, " we mounted our horses, meaning to ride to Dunster, to inform your honour that Master Bachell was not returned to his house, and to ask what we were to do with our prisoners, whom we have left in security. Seeing a crowd assembled here as we rode by, we judged it might be best to jom it, and see the cause of its assembling.

"A mighty fine story, truly," said Mauworth; " the fools have been frightened out of their wits.

" Never trust me again," said Alick Pearson, in a whisper to his master, "if I be wrong in saying that Janet hath done this: she, doubtless unfastened the doors for her fellow-servants, and they, having beaten and scared the knaves to their heart's content, submitted to be shut up again, to make them believe that their tormentors were not mere mortals."

" But the horses? how can you account for the state they were found in?" asked Master Bachell.

"Janet's father, no doubt has been driving them round the pastures, while their riders were being punished within," said Alick.

"Master Bachell," said Pym, " have you a hand in this unseemly business?"

"I was not at my house, as your own men will testify, last night: I passed it at the Castle of Master Luttrell, of which he and others can assure you, and in riding thither, I heard of your detention here, and had it not been so late, and that Master Luttrell had retired, well-nigh worn

out by fatigue, and alarm for the safety of his
ward, I would have aroused him and brought him
to release you on the instant."

" I cannot doubt your word, sir," said Pym, " but
here be matters that must be investigated. 1
will return with you to Ashley-Combe, and will,
if I may make so bold, remain there until I am
furnished with horses, and enabled to return to
Cutcombe."

As a guest, Master Pym shall be welcome to
Ashley-Combe, if he will dismiss his followers, and
place himself under my protection; but as one having
authority from one estate of the realm, in direct
opposition to my sovereign's wishes, I cannot, and
will not admit him within my walls," said Master
Bachell; "my servant's horse is at his service.
Alick, dismount and give place to Master Pym;
you can follow us on foot."

. Pym seemed hesitating how to act, when Mauworth drew his attention to two troopers, each
with a led horse by his side, riding down Dunkery
Hill in a direction from Cutcombe, to where they
were standing. They soon came to the spot, and

L 3

rode up to Pym, presenting him with a packet which bore the seal of the house of commons, and was directed to him and ordered to be delivered with all speed.

Pym broke the seal, skimmed over the contents of the paper, and his eyes glistened as he said to Mauworth, "I must away instantly—there be news, good news; the Scottish covenanters await my presence in London, and the queen's ship, in which she has sent from Holland ammunitions of war, and supplies of money for Charles Stuart, is beset at sea, and likely to be captured. Master Bachell and you Master Luttrell, I must leave you now, for weighty matters call me hence; but rest assured that you shall hear from those, ere long, who will make you sorely repent of conniving at, to say the least—a breach of their authority.

"Fare you well, John Pym," said Master Luttrell, "and do *you* rest assured, that my friend here and myself shall be ready to justify our proceedings when *legally* called upon to do so. Long live the king!"

Amidst the shouts of the Dunster men, and the

groans of the troopers, Pym mounted one of the led horses and Mauworth the other, and rode off towards Cutcombe, followed by the six mounted troopers.

Master Luttrell took his friend Bachell with him to Dunster Castle, making all his retainers follow them, for fear they should fall upon the dismounted troopers, who followed their master on foot to Cutcombe ; the preacher and Roger Priver taking good care to accompany them. Alick Pearson was dispatched to Ashley-Combe to release the prisoners, and report to his fellow-servants all that had occurred.

CHAPTER XV.

HUGH de Mohun and Julian Bachell, wearied·by
the exertions and excitements of the previous
day, slept longer and sounder than was their wont.
They were early risers by habit, but when they
awoke on the morning after the revels at Culbone,
the sun was already high in the heavens. Julian sprung from his bed at once, and dressed himself, but Hugh, who had been busy in dreams,
with the rescue of Prudence Everard from the
waves of the Bristol Channel, turned on his side,
and sought sleep again. He was in hopes that the
visions of his slumbers would return; for it was
just as his fair rescued one was pouring into his
eager ears her thanks for the services which he

had rendered her, that he awoke. He had just sunk again into that pleasant state, when we are not certain whether we are awake or asleep, as his door was opened, and a hand laid upon his shoulder.

" What ho! friend Hugh," said a voice, "arouse thee man, and enjoy the freshness of the morning air."

" Ay—ay, Giles Tudball and Will Bowering— I hear you—I come, I come—hold you but taut upon the haulser, and she shall yet be saved—a few strokes of my right arm will see us on dry land," murmured Hugh, as rearing his left arm aloft, and using his right hand as if in the act of swimming, he turned and raised himself in his bed.

"Why how now, Hugh? art dreaming over again the scenes of yesterday?" asked Julian, as he gazed on the handsome face of his friend.

" Is it you, Julian? I would not use a harsh word to one whom I esteem as I do thee? but I would thou hadst been any where but here, just now; thou hast broken the thread of the pleasantest dream that—"

"Tush man, leave dreams to dreamers, and wake thou to realities: Mistress Prudence Everard, I warrant you, is waiting with her guardian, to repeat the thanks she uttered so freely yesternight, and is perhaps—and it is of more consequence to her, waiting to break her fast: up man," said Julian.

Hugh rose in his bed, and wondered that he was not in his own room in the turret, with his usual means of exchanging his sea dress, for his sober suit of grey, within his reach. Julian was obliged to repeat to him the later transactions of the past night, before he could account for his being in a small sleeping room within the Castle, instead of in his own little closet, over the gateway.

"Thanks, Julian, thanks, I understand my position clearly now, but my mind has been sleepless though my body has not; I have dreamed, Julian, the most delicious—"

"Pooh, pooh, man; banish them, as I said before, for the more pleasing reality," said Julian, as he removed part of the upper bedding, and then threw open the casement of the room.

" But I have nothing to put on save my mumming dress, as Mistress Tudball calls my sea-going suit, and I dare hardly appear before my kind tutor in the clothes that are scarcely yet dry from my truanting yesterday; do summon Basil Chipera, if thou canst, and bid him provide me with a suit more proper to appear in."

" Nay, were I Hugh de Mobun, I should choose rather to present myself to the pretty eyes of Prudence Everard, in the dress wherein she will recognise her preserver, than in a modest suit, more befitting the person of an Oxford student, than one who mastered the old Berkshire stick-player, and the burly butcher in the wrestling ring; and afterwards proved himself so good a swimmer, as to save a fair girl from a watery grave. But if you really are not willing to appear in your damp sailor's dress, here, I will freely give up my forester's suit to you, and don your mumming garments : in good sooth, I would not mind the risk of chills, agues, and rheumatism, to be mistaken for you, if it were but for a few minutes, to enjoy the smiles of gratitude that the fair Prudence will not fail to bestow on one, whom she may, for a short time mistake for her preserver."

"Enough, Julian, enough," said Hugh, "I will join you on the terrace in a few seconds."

Julian smiled significantly as he left his friend, who, in a short period, joined him in the same dress as he had worn on the previous day.

"To the keep—to the keep," said Hugh, "let us enjoy the fresh breezes from the Channel on this lovely morning; they will brace our nerves, and give us fresh life."

As he uttered these words, Hugh fairly raced before his friend up the short ascent that ran round the Castle, and led to the keep. The path was made through a dense mass of elms, which covered three sides of the steep on which the Castle stood. As they bounded along, the rooks, hundreds of whom nestled in the branches above them, left their nests, and flew screaming upwards; but after circling round their homes for a few seconds, settled again, as if aware no enemy was to be dreaded in those secure retreats.

"Here we are, Julian," said Hugh, panting with

the exertions he had made to reach the summit; "here we are, on the loveliest spot in the west of this fair Isle; see, yonder is Grabhurst Hill, that emulates this torr in height, and there is Dunkery, and there Conygar, and below it Minehead, at the foot of lofty Greenaleigh—and there, look there, Julian, is Hone-mouth, and Master Luttrell's little craft, lying as unconcernedly as though her planks had not been in danger of parting company, with each other; and there are the stores of Master Robert Quirke, and, as I believe, Giles Tudball's Blossom of Minehead just setting her sails; and yonder are the Welsh Hills or mountains, as Master Jenkins calls them, and—"

"A truce—a truce, good Hugh—you forget that these scenes are familiar to me, who have been a frequent visitor at Dunster Castle; but see here, Hugh; here down through this vista in the woods, the wheel of the mill of Dunster, dashing the waters of the bright brook that flows from Grabhurst, over its whirling surface. Is it not beautiful, to see through this gloomy grove, the spray sparkling like brilliants, in the gleams of the sunshine below?"

"Beautiful, indeed it is, Julian, and I am not sorry that time has, by its corroding powers, changed what was a huge frowning fortress into a peaceable habitation for rooks and singing birds. Where stately sentinels uttered their watch-words, as the guard went its rounds, or a strange footstep was heard, the nightingale's notes, and the whistling of the blackbird or the mavis are now heard, mingled with the joyful chirrupings of other emulant song birds. Yon crumbling ruins, could doubtless tell some tales of woe and misery, could their disjointed stones but speak."

As he said this, Hugh pointed to the ruins of a round tower, which impended over the Castle and the town, and commanded the hills that surrounded it on every side but the one which looked down upon the marsh-grounds, and the Channel. But little of the building remained ; but what little had not been cleared away, shewed an arched doorway, flanked by walls of enormous thickness, and formed of the dark, red rock, so prevalent in the strata of the neighbouring hills or torrs. Rumor said, that the stones of the fallen walls had been con-

sumed in filling up some gloomy dungeons below
them, and a subterranean cavern, which communicated with the Castle, and thence, by other passages,
with the priory of Dunster, in order that in trou-
blous times, the monks might find a safe retreat
in the Castle.

Julian, leaning on Hugh's shoulder, drew him
gently towards the door of the tower, and pointing to
the remains of the arch, shewed him two shields, each
bearing on its mutilated surface a coat of arms.

" These, Hugh, are said to be the shields of the
whilome owners of Dunster ; you see, though but
faintly, the one on the left, bears, *gule,* a dexter
arm, habited in a maunch, *ermine,* the hand, *proper,*
holding a fleur de lis, *or ;* that on the right, bears
or, a cross engralled, *sable.*"

" I see," said Hugh, " though I confess I am not
curious in heraldry ; I would earn a coat of arms
for myself, rather than be indebted for it to some
ancestor, many generations removed. These, however, I can, even in my ignorance of such matters,
testify are not the arms of the Luttrells, for they,
as you may see, without and within the Castle walls,

bear for their crest, five feathers in a plume, and
for arms, a sable bend between six martlets, having
for supporters, two swans with coronets around
their throats."

"Those Hugh," said Julian seriously, pointing
to the archway, "those are the arms of the Mohuns, formerly owners of this Castle and its demes-
nes, with many fair acres around them : you best
know whether *you* have any claim to wear them."

"Julian Bachell," said Hugh, after a closer examination of the heraldric shields than he had before deigned to bestow upon them, " I know not,
whether or no I am entitled to bear those arms:
a mystery hangs over me, but I care not at present to seek to solve it.   My father, I am told—"

" Nay—nay, Hugh," said Julian, " do not—
do not for a moment fancy that I sought to en-
trap you into the betrayal of any family secrets."

" I do not fancy it; an I did, I should be silent.
My father, I am told, died early in my childhood,
and by violence.   My mother sought to hide
her grief in a foreign land, leaving me to the care
of an old nurse, in my infancy, and afterwards to
my kind friend and tutor Master Robert Snel-

ling, now parson of Dunster. I have that opinion of his judgment and discretion, Julian, that I have never pressed him to relate to me more of my family matters, than he has thought right to impart; but I doubt not, that when he deems it fitting and proper, I shall be made fully acquainted with every circumstance, that it concerns me to know: but who cometh here?"

"Basil Chipera, or my eyes deceive me," said Julian.

The parish clerk and cordwainer of Dunster, sprung lightly up the steps upon the green sward, which led to the keep, and doffing his cap, begged to know, "whether it were the young gentlemens' pleasure to break their fast with the ladies in the hall, or to have a meal served for them, with the chaplain Master Snelling."

"With the ladies, by all means," said both the young men.

"Then follow me, sirs, for the meal is already set out, and Mistress Luttrell and her ward, wait but for my summons to take their seats."

"For *your* summons?" asked Julian; "where then is the butler, that you are acting in his room?"

"May it please you, Master Julian, I am almost the only male domestic left within the walls, for the serving-men were summoned, early in the morning, to act as a body-guard to their master, and his friend Master Bachell of Ashley-Combe, who are—"

"My father—hath he been at Dunster Castle?"

"He arrived late last night, after you had retired, and would not have you disturbed from your rest. He roused my master, at an early hour this morning, with the news that the friends and allies of certain youthful revellers, had taken Master Pym and his followers in a trap, on their way hence to Ashley-Combe, and had shut them up for the night, in the iron mines at the foot of Dunkery Hill."

"And Master Luttrell?" said Hugh.

"Rose, on the instant, and summoning all the servants, and several of the Dunster men, set out with Master Bachell to release them," said Basil.

"And why did he not rouse us? surely our assistance might have been deemed—"

"Your presence might have been productive of bad consequences," said Basil Chipera, "though

Roger Priver had had his warrant torn to shreds, Pym is not one to be trifled with, and hath a strong party to back him."

"Pooh! the Dunster men—I mean the *true* men, could have easily mastered Roger Priver and his comitatus with Pym's trained-bands to boot," said Julian.

"I meant neither comitatus nor trained troopers, when I spoke of Master Pym's having a strong party to back him," said Basil; "I alluded to the parliament, which seems to usurp the powers of the king."

"And do the ladies," asked Hugh de Mohun, "know the cause of their being thus left to the services of Basil Chipera, and the companionship of the two young gentlemen, who have, unwittingly it is true, been the cause of these unpleasant disturbances?"

"Doubtless sir, doubtless; for Mistress Luttrell herself, ordered her tiring-maid to summon you to the meal which I was preparing; but, for certain reasons, I thought I had better relieve her from so onerous a duty, and come myself," said Basil; and

as he said so, he uttered a low, peculiar sound, some
thing between a cough and a laugh.

"What, sirrah!—how mean you? would'st
hint, that Mohun or I, would offer any rudeness to the discreet serving-maid of Mistress Luttrell?"

"Far be it from my thoughts; rudeness? no,
no rudeness, but I thought I might be better able
to supply the information you would require
than"—

"A pretty young woman, whose breath might
have failed her, under the exertion of climbing to
the keep of Dunster Castle," said Hugh.

Basil Chipera gave another of his peculiar
sounds, and then turned and ran rapidly down the
slopes, to the Castle. The young men followed
him more leisurely, and when they entered the
hall, found the ladies already seated at the upper
table, and a few domestics, all of the weaker sex
save Basil Chipera, in attendance upon them.

As Hugh de Mohun approached the table, and
removed his cap, which allowed his luxuriant black
hair to fall over his shoulders, Julian thought him

the handsomest man he had ever seen, and when he removed his eyes from his friend, and turned them on Prudence Everard, he fancied that he read the same opinion in her speaking looks. She looked pale, and as if suffering from the cold and fright of the previous evening; but, when she rose to return her preserver's salutation, the blood mounted to her face, and her eyes beamed so brightly, and so sweet a smile spread itself over her features, that Julian thought, with no little surprise, that, until that moment, he had had no notion Prudence Everard was so very beautiful.

He removed his gaze however, from the preserver and the preserved, to pay his attentions to Mistress Luttrell, who, when she had returned the salutations of the young men, and made kind inquiries after their health, summoned Basil Chipera to his post, and set them an example to commence the morning's meal, which they were not slow to follow.

The meal was eaten nearly in silence, for the table was surrounded by female domestics; but, as soon as it was ended, Mistress Luttrell, leaning on

the arm of Prudence Everard, led the way to the
library, and bade the young men follow her.

" Here is one here, Hugh de Mohun, to whom
it becometh you to apologize humbly for having absented yourself, without permission, from his valuable lectures, and for appearing in a dress, which,
however well it becomes you as a man, is all unseemly for a student.   Master Snelling, if the
book you are pondering over, can spare your earnest gaze for a few seconds, I would pray you to
bestow them in chiding your runaway pupil here,"
said Mistress Luttrell, smiling as she spoke.

" My dear Hugh—my dear Hugh, you are
welcome : I forgive you all the trouble and anxiety
you have cost me—freely forgive you, for
having rescued this dear child here," said the
tutor, taking Prudence Everard by the hand, and
imprinting a kiss upon it. " Had she perished in
the waves, Dunster Castle would have scarcely
again been enlivened by a smile from its mistress."

" True, true, good Master Snelling, in losing
Prudence Everard, I should have felt that I had
lost a daughter ; indeed Hugh, we—that is, I,
cannot be sufficiently grateful for your—"

"Nay, say no more, madam; Julian here, is equally entitled to your praises with myself," said Hugh.

"No," said Julian, sharply; "no, whatever merit is due, is due to you, Mohun. It may be my good fortune to deserve the thanks of Mistress Everard at some future time."

The words uttered by Julian were uttered in so unwonted a tone, that the ladies, Hugh de Mohun, and even the usually absent Master Snelling, could not help looking earnestly at him, to see if anything had ruffled his temper. His cheeks were flushed, and his light blue eyes sparkled proudly, as he turned them first on Prudence Everard, and then upon Hugh de Mohun, who returned his gaze so fixedly, that Julian shrunk abashed from it, and, turning on his heel, sought a distant window, that commanded a view of the town and the approach to the Castle.

Hugh was about to follow him, and demand the meaning of his haughty looks and proud demeanor, but Mistress Luttrell and Prudence, who, by a glance at each other, seemed to have commu-

nicated their thoughts of Julian's conduct and the
consequences that might have resulted from it,
stayed him, and by compelling him to give them and
Master Snelling a long account of the events at
Culbone revels, enabled Julian to recover, partially
it is true, his good-humour. He even supplied several particulars, which Hugh's modesty would not
allow him to recount fully and fairly; but, when
he had done so, as if he had acquitted himself
of a debt due to another, he again turned on his
heel, and sought his former station at the window.

Hugh followed his movements with his eyes:
again the colour rose to his cheeks, and he seemed
bent on demanding of him, on the spot, the meaning of his unusual conduct. Again, a woman's
tact was employed to prevent mischief. Julian
was requested to go with Master Snelling to the
town, and inquire for news of his father and the
party who had accompanied him to the Dunkery
mines.

"I would do your bidding gladly, ladies, and
leave Hugh de Mohun to entertain you further
with a description of our follies, did I not see the

very party, of whom you seek some news, already approaching the Castle. Yonder come Master Luttrell and my father, with the Castle servants, having dismissed the Dunster men at the door of the hostelry, into which they are hurrying, as bees into a hive, doubtless to break their fast at the expense of the lord of this Castle," said Julian.

The sound of horses' hoofs on the hard, rocky road, leading up to the gates, was shortly heard, and, in a few minutes, Master Luttrell and Julian's father entered the library, and briefly recounted the result of their interview with Pym. They then sought refreshment in the hall, whither they bade the two young men follow them, leaving Mistress Luttrell and Prudence Everard to the companionship of the parson of Dunster.

Master Bachell seemed inclined to be severe upon his son for the part he had taken in the revels, but Hugh de Mohun generously exonerated him from all blame, by explaining the means to which he had resorted to induce him to be his companion. In this he was aided by Master Luttrell, who, good-

humouredly rated Hugh on his imprudence, and
bade him, who had been the sole cause of all
the difficulties and dangers likely to result from
his wild thoughtlessness, suggest some means of
appeasing the wrath of Pym, and compensating
Roger Priver and the preacher for the ill-treatment to which they had been subjected.

"I alone have been to blame," said Hugh, "and
upon me alone let the anger of Pym and the
wrath of Priver and Master Browne fall."

" Whatever punishment the parliament, by its
orders, inflicts upon Mohun, I share at any and
all risks," said Julian · " it never shall be said,
that a Bachell yielded to another in generosity;
even though that other be a stranger, and altogether
unknown, except as the pupil of a good man and
a protégé of the owner of this Castle."

"Why how now?" said Julian's father, looking
searchingly at his son, "do you, Julian, call your
friend Hugh there a stranger, and allude to a
Mohun as an unknown? what means this? It
seems to me, that, since I left Ashley-Combe yester-
morn, madness has seized upon every one."

" What the young Master Bachell may mean, I know not," said Hugh; " but within this half-hour, he seems to me to have taken up a tone and manner as insulting to me as they are unaccountable. If he hath cause of quarrel, let him state it, he shall not find me backward in—"

" Tush, boy, tush !—if Julian's temper be soured, the point of your rapier, or a ball from one of your play-thing pistols, will not sweeten it," said Master Bachell.

" Nor those haughty looks, with which you eye your friend," said Master Luttrell: " but what means it all, Hugh ? I pray you explain."

" I know not what it means, nor have I any explanation to offer," said Hugh, " I pray you, inquire of the young Master Bachell, what cause of quarrel I have given him."

" Julian, what does all this mean ?" asked his father.

" Nay, ask Mohun; he can best tell why he treats me with such looks, and even offers to back his haughty demeanor towards me with his arms. I have no quarrel with him," said Julian.

" Nor have I any quarrel with you, Julian. I cannot, in any way, account—"

" Then shake hands and be friends again, if you have been foes, even in imagination," said Master Bachell.

Julian extended his hand, and Mohun took it, but each felt, that the gripe of the other was different from what he had always hitherto found it, and each sat silently apart, during the discussion that followed between the seniors, as to the best mode of being prepared to meet the accusations that would be brought against them by Pym. After a lengthened conversation, it was agreed, that Master Bachell and Julian should return to Ashley-Combe, and there, quietly and in secrecy, arm their followers; while Master Luttrell was pursuing the same plan with the tenants and retainers of the Castle ; and that each should give the other notice if any danger impended over him, and both be prepared for mutually assisting and protecting each other.

The council, if such the little meeting might be called, was then broken up, and, after having taken

leave of the ladies, Master Bachell and Julian, mounted on one of Master Luttrell's horses, left the Castle
followed at a respectful distance by Alick Pearson.

When they had left Dunster town, and were passing under the dark boughs of the pines which
covered the sides of Conygar hill, his father rode
close to Julian's side, and inquired of him,
firmly, but kindly, the meaning of the tone he had
assumed, and the rude allusions he had made to
one, whom, for some months past, he had proudly
acknowledged as a friend.

Julian tried to evade giving an answer to his
father's questions, by saying, that he had merely
followed an example set him by Hugh ; but, upon
being closely examined and pressed home, he at
last owned, that he felt offended by the looks and
tones bestowed by Prudence Everard upon one com-
paratively a stranger to her ;—so much kinder and
softer, than she had ever cast upon him, whom she
had known for many years.

" And so, young man, because a fair girl allows
her eyes to beam kindly upon a youth who saved
her life at the risk of his own, and thanks him for

his timely succour, in warmer and softer tones than she bestows upon a mere acquaintance of her infancy, you must needs feel offended, and vent your spleen upon one, whom you should feel proud to call your friend," said Master Bachell.

"I shall call him so no longer, unless he apologizes for his haughty looks and inflated demeanor A Bachell is not to be insulted by a mere stranger, and one who knows so little of his own origin, as not to be able to recognize the arms borne by those of his own name when he sees them," replied Julian.

"Talk not so foolishly, Julian," said his father; "though a mystery may, for a time, hang over the birth of Hugh de Mohun, he will at some future period, prove his right to wear the arms earned by his ancestors, or bravely win, in the field of battle, heraldic honours for himself."

"A deed not so easy of accomplishment, as the mere dragging of a timid maiden from the troubled waters of a shallow stream," said Julian.

"Fie, Julian, fie—you are mad, or jealous, or both. Curb your temper, lest I repent me of the

indulgences, which, as the only child of thy long
lost mother, I have, too weakly perchance, bestowed upon you."

Julian did not answer his father; but put spurs
to his horse, and rode forward in silence, until they
reached Ashley-Combe. He alighted at the hall
door, threw his bridle to Alick Pearson, and sought
his sleeping-room, where he exchanged his disguise for his usual morning suit. He then summoned Janet, the lodge-keeper's daughter, and
learnt from her the method by which she, assisted by the servants, had so greatly alarmed Pym's
stalwart troopers, after drugging their night-possets.

But we must leave Ashley-Combe, and return
to Dunster Castle.

As soon as the Bachells had left the Castle,
Master Luttrell took Hugh de Mohun aside, and
inquired of him the cause of the evident displeasure of Julian, and his own proud looks of defiance.

Hugh answered, and answered truly, that he
could not account, in any way, for Julian's conduct, unless it arose from a feeling, now that their
folly was over, that, by his persuasions, he had been

induced to take such a share in the forbidden sports
and pastimes as would eventually bring himself and
his father into danger and perhaps disgrace. He
freely owned that he had been wrong in resenting
his friend's intemperate conduct, and promised to
be more guarded for the future.

Master Luttrell kept his eye fixed on the countenance of Hugh, while he answered him ; and
was convinced, from every look and lineament,
that he had not tried to deceive him, and that he
really knew of no cause, beyond the one he had
suggested, for Julian's display of ill-temper.   He
left him, therefore, with a request that he would
resume his ordinary dress, and join the family at
the dinner-table, at noon.

Hugh de Mohun gladly availed himself of an
opportunity for retiring for a while : he was anxious to learn from some of his companions of the
previous day the particulars of the attack on
Pym and the Puritans, and to ascertain what their
plans were for the future ; in order to avoid the
punishment which Pym and his party in parliament would doubtless inflict upon those, who had

so rudely set their orders at defiance and torn up their warrant.

He did not wish to pass through the town of Dunster, for many reasons, in his present costume; and, as he had left his usual every-day dress with Dame Tudball, it was necessary that he should go to Minehead to resume it; for he felt convinced, from his knowledge of the dame's temper, that she would not give up his clothes to any one but himself, and then, not without reading him a severe lecture on his folly, in having got into a scrape himself, and led her husband and Will Bowering to join him. He sought the lodge, and gained his own room, whence he let himself down, by the aid of the ivy stems, into the thicket below the gate tower. A few rapid strides brought him to the edge of the lower park, the fence of which he cleared at a bound, and, without seeing any one or being seen, gained the meadows at the back of the hostel called the Luttrell Arms.

He cautiously approached the house, and learnt from the host that Dr. Graveboys and Jansen had quitted the town, soon after they had heard from

Basil Chipera that Pym and his followers were likely to be set at liberty; and were then some miles on their road towards Bristol, where, it was reported, some pestilent disorder was raging, which the mediciner thought not unlikely to furnish him with numerous customers.

Hugh, having learnt all the information that the host could furnish him with, again entered the park, and quickly sought the marshes below it. Through these he hurried, avoiding Alcombe and the upper town of Minehead, and so reached the residence of Giles Tudball, which was at the bottom of the town, and close to a lane leading down to the marshes and the shore. He looked about the out-premises, where the skins and hides were dressed and dried, in hopes of seeing Giles before he sought his wife; that he might learn what sort of mood the dame was in, and what kind of reception she had given her husband, on his return from Dunster.

Neither Giles, however, nor any of his men were to be seen; so Hugh had no other course to pursue, but to knock at the door of the dwelling-house, and ask for Dame Tudball.

"Keep the outside, keep the outside, Master Hugh, not a footfall of yours shall ever be heard within these doors again;" screamed the dame from her window above him.

"My good dame, what have I done to offend you?" said Hugh, with a sorrowful face, and in humble tones.

"Don't good me, or dame me—or speak to me—you, you ne'er-do-well—is it not enough that you make a fool of yourself by your mummings, and your junketings, and your wrestlings, and other ungodly sports, but you must lead my good man—fool that he is—into scrapes and fightings, and perhaps into prison? Get you gone, and never let me see the face of you more."

When the dame had uttered these words as rapidly as she could, she shut the casement with such force, that two or three quarries of glass were shaken from their frames, and came crashing on the ground at Hugh's feet.

"See there again," shouted the dame through the vacant leads, "ill-luck attends you, wherever you come or go, and I hope it will bide by you for life—I do."

" Nay, good, kind dame, mind not this trifle, I will send one that shall soon repair the damage at my cost; and my good dame, do just tell me where I may see Giles, for I have news for him, and let me in to exchange these garments for my student's dress," said Hugh.

The dame left the casement for a few seconds and then returned to it, and when she had opened it, she threw out Hugh's clothes in a bundle, and bade him " trudge elsewhere with them; for into her house he should never set foot again."

" And will you not tell me where I may see Giles, dame? his safety may depend on ' my seeing him," said Hugh.

" Safety? and what care I for his safety? he may as well be in a prison as junketing in an ale-house, instead of being at home with his wife and attending to his business.'"

" Is he at the Plume of Feathers in the upper town, or at—"

" If you want him, you may seek him, and the search will not be a hard one, to one who knows his haunts and habits," said the offended lady, again closing the casement, but with less violence than before.

Hugh did not wait to see if the dame would repent, and let him in to change his dress, but sought the stable, and, mounting the ladder leading to the hay-loft above it, converted it into a dressing-room, and, when he had changed his clothes, he hid his sailor's dress behind some bundles of fodder. He then returned to the beach, and, following its windings, gained the pier, and entered the Ship-aground, at its head. There he found Giles, Will Bowering, and several more, listening to Richard Luckes and his wife, who had not long returned home from Ashley-Combe, and were entertaining their friends and customers with an account of all that had taken place there, previously to their return.

Hugh de Mohun seated himself amongst them, and, when they had exchanged all the information they were possessed of or required, it was agreed that no further steps should be taken in the business, until they should hear, which they would doubtless do, through Master Luttrell or Master

Bachell, what means of punishment Pym, and
the parliament, at his instigation, would adopt.

This agreement was sealed by a tankard of foaming ale, of which all partook largely but the old
harbour-master, who, complaining of its being somewhat cold to his stomach, was furnished with some
strong waters, at the expense of Master Robert
Quirke.

Hugh then withdrew, taking Giles Tudball with
him, and, as soon as they had gained the beach,
gave him so vivid a description of the reception he
had met with from the dame, and the sort of humour she was in, that Giles determined to set out
upon one of those inland expeditions, in which he
frequently indulged under various pretences.

Hugh tried to dissuade him from doing so, lest
his prolonged absence should make his good
woman more irate; but Giles knew that, if he allowed it time, her temper would cool, especially if
he made good use of his absence, and returned
home with a full purse.

Hugh, therefore left him, after he had told him
to let Will Bowering seek for and take care of his

sea-suit and retraced his steps to Dunster Castle, whither he arrived, without any one but Basil Chipera knowing of his absence, in good time for the mid-day meal.

CHAPTER XVII.

MASTER Thomas Luttrell and Master Bachell,
were busily engaged in preparing such of their tenants as were of age to bear arms, in the exercise
of the pike, rapier, and pistol.   The men were furnished with horses, and mustered regularly on
certain days, and not dismissed until they had performed certain evolutions on horseback, and certain
exercises on foot, which were deemed necessary by
their respective officers. So great was the zeal dis-
played, especially by the younger men, who thoroughly hated and detested the Roundheads, that a
few weeks sufficed to render many a hand, which had
hitherto only guided a plough or wielded a whip,
fully capable of managing a pike, and using the

small-sword and heavier cavalry sabre. The neighbouring gentry too, who had heard of the proceedings at Culbone revels and their results, followed the example set them by the lords of Dunster
and Ashley-Combe, with whom they lived on the
most friendly terms, and armed their tenants and
dependents. A little army was thus formed and
prepared to defend themselves and their leaders,
against any hostile measures on the part of Master
John Pym of Cutcombe, or King Pym,—a title
by which he had then become generally known.

These warlike precautions, however, seemed to
be unnecessary; for nothing was heard either of
Pym or the Parliament, with reference to the illegal acts of the Culbone revellers, or the imprisonment of the constables by the Dunster men. Pym
and the Parliament were, in fact, too much busied
with affairs of State, to find time to think of so trifling a matter as a breach of their authority in a
little, out-of-the-way nook, in the West. Pym
was engaged in daily conferences with the Scottish covenanters, and in laying their complaints
and wishes before the house of commons. The
commons were occupied in receiving messages

from the king, who was then at York, and in fram-
ing such answers as should involve him deeper and
deeper in the meshes of a policy, which, they began
to see, would end in open rebellion, and the curtail-
ment, if not the utter extinction, of the regal
power. The royalist members, few in number, but
all good men, and true to their sovereign, vainly endeavoured to stem the tide of treason, flowing in so
fiercely against them. They formed but a miser-
able minority, and their voices, when raised in defence of their lawful sovereign, were drowned by the
overwhelming shouts of his opponents. Many of
them, who foresaw that words would lead, and
shortly too, to blows, left London for their country
homes, where they either levied forces to be in
readiness for the approaching struggle, or, having collected all their serviceable followers, joined
the king as speedily as they could.

Pym had not forgotten the insults he had met
with at Culbone and Dunster : he bided his time,
thinking that an opportunity would shortly occur
of punishing those with greater severity than he
could do at present, who had despised his authority
and imprisoned himself and his followers.

Had he been inclined to be oblivious on the subject, he had those about him who did not fail to refresh his memory. The preacher, Robert Browne, and the bailiff of Dunster, Roger Priver, had positively refused to return to their homes, until such measures had been carried into effect as should ensure them from further vengeance from the malignants of Dunster and its neighbourhood. Pym, not choosing to leave them at Cutcombe, lest the unrestrained licentiousness of their speech should provoke an attack, that might endanger the safety of his family, bade them follow him to London, and upon their arrival, appointed Master Browne to be the private chaplain to his household, and Roger Priver to act as superintendent, or officer, over a small body of men, whom he had armed and kept about his person. Pym was a courageous man, and belonged to a party that was in favour, especially with the lower orders of London and Westminster; but, since the very prominent part he had taken in procuring the execution of Strafford, he had, more than once, been attacked in his passage from his residence to the house of commons. He had defended himself bravely and successfully against these attacks; but his friends, who knew his value to the cause they were advocating, had prevailed upon him to make the assurance of his safety doubly sure by going down to Westminster, surrounded by such a body of men as should deter his enemies —who, of course were called the myrmidons of Charles Stuart, papistical malignants—from making further aggressions on his person.

Like Xerxes, with his minister by his side, bidding him daily, to 'Remember the Athenians,' Pym was daily reminded by his chaplain and the officer of his body-guard not to forget the malignants of Dunster and Ashley-Combe.

" How long? how long?" would Master Browne cry, as he raised his eyes to the ceiling, at the conclusion of his graces before and after meat, " How long? how long shall the men of Duntser and of Porlock triumph ungodly?"

" How long? how long—will the parliament permit its officer's ill-treatment, and the destruction of its warrant of authority, by the hand of prelatists and papists, to go unpunished?" would Roger Priver Snuffle daily into his master's ears, as he rode by his side down to the house of commons.

Pym could do no more to appease the eagerness of his followers, than to bid them have patience, until weightier matters were disposed of; a reply that invariably produced a deep groan from the breasts of those, who were panting for vengeance on their foes, and whose hatred grew the fiercer, the longer the execution of their vengeance was delayed.

But we must leave London and public events for the present, and return to Dunster Castle.

Although Master Luttrell was much occupied in levying and training his troops, he was not unmindful of the promise that he had made to Hugh de Mohun, that his ward, the fair Prudence Everard, should represent on canvass her escape from the waters of the Hone river. Prudence was skilful in painting, and, as Mistress Luttrell was constantly by her side, when Hugh sat for his portrait, she could see nothing objectionable or improper in the execution of the pleasing task which her guardian had set her. The picture proceeded but slowly, it is true; for the palette was frequently laid aside for a ramble in the gardens, or on the keep;

—for a gallop over the park and the surrounding
Tors; but still more frequently, for the enjoyment
of conversation and music,—an art in which
also Prudence excelled. Still it progressed,
to the satisfaction of good Master Luttrell, who,
though by no means a connoisseur in the art of
limning, could not fail to acknowledge his fair
ward's success in representing on the canvass the
features of her preserver.

To Hugh de Mohun, these days passed as if
they had been a succession of joyous dreams. His
worthy tutor, Robert Snelling, was too busily engaged in writing a treatise in defence of the imprisoned Laud, to devote much of his time to his pupil's improvement. He, therefore, contented himself with pointing out to him such passages in
the ancient poets and historians as he wished
him to study during the day, and Basil Chipera,
did not deem it any part or portion of his duty
to inform the tutor, that the pupil was so re-
markably quick at study, as to be able to conquer
the difficulties of his authors in a very short space
of time.

Master Luttrell was, as we have seen, much employed in training his followers, and Mistress Luttrell had many duties to attend to, in her nursery, and in other parts of her establishment, besides watching the growing attachment of two young persons, or rather of exercising a duenna-like *surveillance* over them, lest an attachment should be formed between a young orphan girl entrusted to her charge, and a young man, of whose origin and prospects in life she was by no means fully informed. Hugh de Mohun and Prudence Everard were, therefore, left much together—but not alone; for the little Alice Luttrell, a lovely child, about twelve years of age, and her brother William, about a twelvemonth younger than she was, were almost constantly their companions, both in the library and in their walks and rides.

It happened one day, some three weeks after the doings recorded in the commencement of our tale, that Hugh de Mohun rode with Prudence Everard to a spot in the park of Dunster, which was a favourite resort of theirs, although it bore but an ill name with the superstitious peasantry

around. On the side of a hill, named **Grabhurst,**
stood a bright, clear pool of water, called St. **Leo**-
nard's Well. It was partly enclosed by a stone wall,
and roofed over, to protect it from the inroads of
the deer and the cattle, which would have polluted,
by their trampling, the pure stream that supplied the town and Castle with water. The walls
and roof were thickly covered with luxuriant ivy,
and around it, grew a circle of lofty trees, which
extended their mighty branches about them, as
if to shelter and protect the humbler thorns, which
flourished beneath their shade.

The waters of St. Leonard's Well were reputed
to be possessed of healing powers; if drunk or
used externally, at their pure source, they were said
to stay fevers and to prevent blindness. It was,
however, necessary to invoke the aid of St. Leonard, before using or drinking of the waters of his
fountain, and that too, either before the sun's rays
had shone upon them, or after they had ceased
to reflect his beams. Early in the morning or late
in the evening, the water was efficacious; but, if
taken when the glare of day was upon it, it lost

its healing properties. Many, who would have gladly tested the medicinal powers of St. Leonard's Well, were deterred from doing so by a story that was current in the neighbourhood, that Mistress Leckey, " the grey woman of Minyead," had of late taken it under her especial protection, and taken up her abode within the grove that surrounded it. The few peasants, more resolute than their friends, who had ventured to drink there at the prescribed hours, had heard strange noises amidst the trees, and seen something grey hovering about the thick may-bushes. Some had even gone so far as to assert, that they had distinctly seen, and been plainly spoken to, by the grey woman, who bade them, as they valued her pleasure or displeasure, not venture a second time to disturb her in her quiet retreat.

In spite of these reports, Hugh de Mohun and Prudence Everard made frequent visits to the well of St. Leonard; for the ride thither was over green, velvety turf, and the view from it was very beautiful. They could tether their ponies to the thorn-bushes, and allow them to crop the luxuriant grass that grew around them; and, seated on the stones, that formed the entrance to the well, enjoy the prospect about them, while the little Alice and her brother amused themselves by gazing at the pebbles, which shone like diamonds, at the bottom of the bright, and bubbling stream-head.

It was on one of the loveliest evenings of that "sweetest month of all the year"—May—when de Mohun and Miss Everard, arriving after a gentle canter at the grove which surrounded the well, dismounted from their forest ponies, and fastened them by their bridles to one of the numerous thorns that grew there. The children dismounted too; but, after amusing themselves, for a short time, by plucking the may-boughs, now covered with their bloom, mounted again, without the knowledge of their friends, and set off for a race upon the soft, noiseless turf. Prudence seated herself on one of the stones at the entrance of the conduit, and de Mohun stood by her side, leaning his back against the dark green leaves and tortuous branches of the ivy, that completely covered the little building. Neither spoke for some miuntes, for both were engaged in viewing the lovely

and extensive prospect before them, and in listening to the nightingales and other song birds, that
were warbling their evening hymns in the thicket
adjoining.

" I wonder, de Mohun," said Prudence Everard,
at length breaking silence, and pointing with her
riding wand towards the Channel, " I wonder if what
I have read of foreign lands be true. Can southern
France, the banks of the Rhine, or the shores of
the pure-skied Italy, so much surpass in beauty
the prospect which now lies before us ?"

" I can scarcely think it," replied Hugh, "and yet,
I have imagined it, when reading the glowing des-
criptions of those who have travelled in the lands,
and about the spots you name. Never have I, I
must confess it, seen this and other spots so beautiful as within these last few days ;—it must be this
splendid weather, that causes every thing to look
so bright and beautiful."

Prudence Everard sighed slightly as she owned
that she too, in her frequent visits to Dunster
Castle, had never seen the country around look so
lovely as it had lately appeared to her.

"See there," said Hugh, pointing over Minehead towards the broad ocean, "see there, where
the setting sun throws its deep red glare over the
calm and placid waters of the Channel, in which we
may fancy reflected as pure a sky as Italy can boast
of. And see here again, to the right, where its
last rays bring out boldly, in relief, the deep recesses and tall forests of our Tors, which need
not yield in height or majesty to the much vaun-
ted hills of Rhineland. Below us too, is a quiet
scene, such as southern France cannot, methinks,
with all her beauties, greatly surpass: of vines and
olives we cannot boast; but those rich sea-green
meads, surrounded by lofty elms and oaks, and
dotted here and there, with flocks and herds, and
the bright green ribbons of the springing corn, pos-
sess such charms for English eyes, that I, for one,
would not willingly exchange them, for what may be
but the fabled glories of other and strange lands."

"Can those other strange lands, of which you
speak, show us any thing more majestic in its simple grandeur than our Castle there, with its dark
red turrets clearly defined against that cloudless

sky; and Conygar too,—its pine-clad sides may fairly emulate, though not upon so grand a scale, the sombre groves of northern England. It is *very* beautiful;" said Prudence Everard.

" It is very, very beautiful," repeated Hugh, and yet the time has not long passed, since I was willing,—ay and anxious,—to exchange these our lovely home-views, and hitherto peaceful lands, for other countries and far different scenes. Now, methinks, I would not leave this happy spot,—this quiet, calm life—for worlds of wealth, or the proudest titles which fame could confer upon me. Would that I were the owner of these fair domains!"

" And why?" said Prudence, turning her dark blue eyes inquiringly on her companion.

" Miss Everard," answered Hugh, as he took the hand which rested on an ivy branch by his side, " if I were the lord of these domains, and master of this fair hand, I would not exchange positions with—"

" Nay—nay, my friend—for such I may innocently call my preserver—" said Prudence Everard, rising, and endeavouring to withdraw her hand, "this is language to which I must not,—cannot listen. Remember de Mohun, I am young—an orphan, and, as I believe, dependent on the bounties of my friends—nay, leave me, I entreat you—release my hand."

" Miss Everard—Prudence Everard, hear me but one word. I love you—love you, with all the fervour of a heart in which passion has never yet held sway—with all the purity of a virgin affection —nay, turn not away until you have heard me out. Never again will I alarm you with an offer of my love—never entreat you to own an affection for me, until I can do so fairly and honourably, and with the obtained sanction of your friends and guardians. A cloud hangs over me at present, which I will speedily dispel, and when I have as-certained and obtained my rank and fortune, both shall be laid at your feet. Tell me— tell me I entreat you, if de Mohun proves himself of un-blemished descent, and the owner of goodly lands, will Miss Everard entrust the happiness of her future years to his keeping?"

"Never—never! the base-born never can be united to the last of the noble Everards."

These words were spoken in a deep, yet shrill voice, which seemed to proceed from the very centre of the well. They were spoken slowly and distinctly—word by word—almost syllable by syllable. Prudence Everard stood still, and turned as pale as the waters at her feet. Hugh de Mohun dropped the hand he held, and gazed into the recesses of the well, as if he expected to find some one concealed within them. It was unoccupied, save by the bubbling waters. He passed rapidly round the building, and then rushed into the grove which surrounded it. No human being was within sight.

"The children!—Alice—William—the children! de Mohun, where are they?"

"Here we are, dear Prudence," said little Alice, "we have had a race, and my dear Sylvia has beaten Willy's Trotty—oh, so much, you cannot think."

"Ay, but your Sylvia is higher by a hand, than poor Trotty, and you had the best start," said the boy.

" Saw you no one near us, as you rode down to the well ?" asked Hugh.

" No one," said Alice. " Indeed, if any one had been at the well, we could not have seen them."

" Why not, dearest ?" asked Prudence Everard.

" Oh," said Willy, " there was a grey sort of mist all about it, that at a distance, looked for all the world like an old woman in a grey cloak."

" We had better return home, Miss Everard," said Hugh : " the evening dew is rising."

Prudence, declining the proffered assistance of de Mohun, mounted the pony, and the party rode, almost in silence, to Dunster Castle.

CHAPTER XVIII.

IT was nearly dark when Hugh de Mohun parted with Prudence Everard and the children, at the small postern, which led from the quadrangle in front of the Castle to the long range of stabling. He did not bid them farewell for the night, as he intended to join them at the supper-table. Supper, that most sociable of all meals, for it is partaken of after the cares and labours of the day are over,—was served about eight o'clock; and the children were not unfrequently allowed to sit up and partake of it, especiallv if they could engage the interest of Prudence Everard as a canvasser in their favour.

Hugh was not a little chafed in his temper, at Miss Everard's having declined his services to assist her from her saddle: a few moments

however, sufficed to enable him to smooth his
ruffled brow.   As he rode homewards, by the side
of her he loved, the words of the mysterious voice
at the well had rung in his ears, and given rise to
thoughts more painful than had ever pervaded his
mind before.   He had endeavoured to bring to his
recollection all the scenes of his earliest days.
He tried to remember the features of those who
were around him in his infancy; but, beyond a
shadowy outline of a tall, dark lady, who had once
or twice received him into her bosom from the
arms of his old nurse, and the dim features of
another domestic, no impressions remained on
his memory.

Was he base-born? how should he solve the
problem?   His aged nurse was he knew not where.
She might be buried for all he knew, and, with
her, the secret of his birth.   His tutor, Master
Snelling, was doubtless furnished with full information on the subject; but was he at liberty to dis-
close what he knew?—He would seek him and
question him closely.

Acting upon this resolve, Hugh, when he had

quitted his companions, crossed the quadrangle, and, with impatient strides, rushed down the steep pathway which led to the gate tower, wherein his tutor lodged. The arched door-way, which gave access to the interior, and was usually open, was now closed, and the door itself fastened. Hugh knocked impatiently upon it with the butt of his riding-whip, but could obtain no reply to his summons. Again and again, and with increasing loudness, were the blows repeated, but to no purpose. He looked up to the window of the room in which his tutor usually studied and wrote, but no light shone from its quarried casement; he went to the farther side of the tower, and, climbing to his own window, by means of the strong ivy stems, tried to gain access to his apartment in his usual way ; but the iron-bound casement was securely fastened within, and he was forced to descend without accomplishing his object. He then, knocked and shouted at a small aperture, which gave light to the lower room, usually occupied by Basil Chipera; but no response was granted to him.

Bestowing any thing but a benediction on the

head of the absent warder, he returned hastily
to the Castle, not doubting that Basil had left
his post for the hostelry in the town, and that he
should find his tutor busily engaged in the library ; a spot that held out so many temptations to
the good old man, that, when once he was ensconced within its walls, Master Chipera knew that
his absence for some hours would not be noticed,
a circumstance by which he did not fail frequently
to profit.

A small side door from the gardens, of which
he had a key, admitted him to a passage leading to
the library.   He opened the inner door, but found
the room in total darkness.   Well knowing the
localities, he crossed it, and made his way to the
entrance hall, and thence to the large hall, or ban-
queting room, where he found several of the servants preparing for the evening meal.   To his inquiries for his tutor, he was answered, that Master
Snelling had set off that afternoon, with Basil Chipera as a servant and guard, for the good city of
Bristol, with the purpose of having his volumi-
nous manuscripts in defence of Laud and the

Church put into print; and had left word that Hugh de Mohun should employ himself in the library, and take up his residence within the Castle, until his return.

Great was the disappointment, but the young man bore it manfully ; for he was aware that his tutor's absence would not be prolonged beyond the ensuing Saturday, as his duties would require his presence on the Sunday. He took a rapid walk on the terrace of the gardens, to allay his irritated feelings; and, when calmness was restored to his mind, he joined the family of his friend at the supper table, with an unbeating heart and unruffled forehead.

" I wonder," said Mistress Luttrell " that Julian Bachell hath been so long an absentee from these walls, which in his childhood were to him as a second home."

" He has been, and is still, busied in assisting his father in raising the tenantry, and perfecting them in their exercises," said Master Luttrell. " King Charles has not a more zealous soldier, in his dominions, than the young Julian. Did he consider his father safe in his absence, he would ere this, have joined the armies already raised in the North, and rallying round their ill-used sovereign."

"An it please you, sir," said the aged butler, as he stood behind his master's high-backed chair, "Master Julian was at the Castle this afternoon."

"And why came he not in, as was his wont?" inquired the lady.

"An it please you, madam, he was about to dismount; but when I told him that Master Hugh de Mohun was absent, riding in the park with Mistress Everard, he turned his horse's head, intending, as I deemed, to join them."

"Saw you nought of him?" asked Master Luttrell

"We did not see him," replied Hugh, "But he might easily have missed us had he sought us; for Dunster park is no paddock to be traversed over in some hour or so."

"Had he ridden to Grabhurst, we must have seen him," said Alice, "for Willy and I were cantering about on the highest ridges of it, while dear Prudence here, and Master Hugh, were amusing themselves by sitting and watching the trickling waters of St. Leonard's Well."

The colour rose vividly in the cheeks of Hugh and Prudence Everard at this simple remark, their eyes met for a moment, and were then firmly fixed on the cloth that covered the board. Mistress Luttrell glanced from one to the other and then at her husband; but her looks were not heeded by the latter, as he was busily employed with the viands before him; and an observation " that Master Bachell had doubtless failed to find his friend de Mohun and ridden home again," put an end to further speculation on the subject.

Supper over, Master Luttrell requested Prudence to take her seat at the instrument, and sing to him one of his favourite songs. She readily complied; but did not sing with her usual spirit. In a duet with Hugh de Mohun, which they had so often sung together as to be perfect in it, Prudence sang in so flat a tone, and the voices were so far from harmonizing, that Mistress Luttrell could not refrain from asking her ward if she were ill.

Prudence owned that she did not feel quite well, and feared she might have taken a slight cold, from riding in the evening dews.

Mistress Luttrell kissed the fair cheek of her
ward, as she stood beside her, and, in a whisper, told her that she thought such late and distant rides had better not be repeated; and then
bade her seek relief from her indisposition in sleep.

Prudence retired immediately, and Hugh would
fain have done so too, for his quick ear had caught
the whispered advice of Mistress Luttrell; but
he was detained for some two tedious hours,
listening to the unentertaining detail, anent the
progress made in military matters by his newly
raised troop, delivered by his host, between the
puffs of his silver-mounted pipe.

The harangue, however, ended with the third
pipe, and Hugh, after having learned that the parson of Dunster would return from Bristol so soon
as he had seen his manuscript placed in the prin-
ter's hands, and given the necessary directions for
having the proof sheets forwarded to him, retired
to his bed, to think over the events of the day.

When Prudence Everard had reached her sleeping room, she dismissed her maid immediately;
declining her services for the night, under the

pléa of a violent head-ache. When the maid had left her, however, she did not commence her preparations for retiring to rest, but sat down near the window, and gently opened the casement. The fresh air from without blew chilly upon her, but the very chilliness was a relief to her. Her brain seemed heated, her forehead throbbed, and the coolness of the night wind spread refreshingly over her temples, and seemed to allay their painful throbbings.

She sat for some time, thinking of the interview with Hugh de Mohun at St. Leonard's Well, and of the strange voice and words, which had closed it so fearfully and abruptly. Maiden-like, she blushed, though no eye was near to see her, when she thought of the sudden declaration of love poured into her ear by her preserver, and resolutely examined her heart, to see if its pure recesses harboured more than a friendly and grateful feeling towards him.

What the result of the self-imposed examination might have been, it is impossible to say; for, ere it came to a conclusion, the fair girl felt a hand laid gently on her shoulder, and heard the gentle voice of her guardian and more than mother whis-per a chiding into her ear, for endangering her health by exposing herself to the damp dews of night.

"Nay, dearest madam," said Prudence, raising Mistress Luttrell's hand to her lips, "no harm will befall me from these pure breezes; indeed they have done me good already, for my head did ache and—"

"Art sure, dearest, that this little heart is not more affected than the head?" said Mistress Lut-trell, drawing her to her, and placing her arm round her slender waist, so that her hand rested on her heart.

Prudence tried to withdraw from her embrace, but her guardian, using a gentle violence, held her firmly, while she questioned her in a low voice, as to what had passed between her and Hugh de Mohun, at the fountain of St. Leonard.

After a slight struggle with herself, Prudence revealed, ingenuously, every thing that had pas-sed between them; and so vividly was the scene impressed upon her memory, that the very words used by Hugh and herself at the well, were repeated to the attentive ear of her guardian.

"I have been to blame," said Mistress Luttrell, as she released the blushing girl from her embrace, and drew her upon a couch by her side; "I only have been to blame: I ought to have been aware of and guarded against the danger of leaving two young hearts, ignorant of the world and of themselves, to the influence of a passion, likely to be engendered by gratitude for a life preserved on the one hand, and on the other, by a noble, a manly feeling of satisfaction, at having been the preserver of so fair a form as this."

Prudence Everard threw herself on Mistress Luttrell's bosom and sobbed.

"Yet why should I blame myself? Prudence Everard, I feel for you as a mother would feel: I do not believe that my love for mine own child, my youthful Alice, surpasses the love I feel for you,—you, who, motherless and fatherless, an orphan indeed, are left to my protection. Were Alice arrived at your time of life, and had she been

preserved from almost certain death by so noble a
youth as Hugh de Mohun, could I—"

"But the words—those fatal, mysteriously
uttered words—'base-born,' can they be true, dearest lady?" said Prudence, raising her face and
gazing fixedly at her guardian.

"Imagination, dearest,—fancy—must have deceived you," said Mistress Luttrell.

"Nay, lady, I heard them pronounced too slowly
and distinctly, ever to attribute them to fancy or
imagination," said Prudence.

"Some prying spy must have been at hand, and
maliciously or playfully, uttered them, in order
to alarm you."

"Not so—it is impossible; you know the spot
well; excepting the rock-covered well itself, and
the small group of trees and bushes which sur-
round it, all is open hill about it, there is not so
much as a thicket to hide a hare, within half a
mile of it," said Prudence, earnestly.

"And may not the recess of the well, or the
overhanging mound, have concealed some wandering eaves-dropper?"

"No, dearest madam, for Hugh de Mohun examined both, speedily and accurately; and the children, who were returning to us at the moment, must have seen any one who had fled from the spot, which was found uninhabited by aught, save ourselves," said Prudence.

"Well, dearest, well," said Mistress Luttrell, "I have no superstitious feelings myself, neither I think, have you. I have no doubt that we shall find some earthly solution of the difficulty which now puzzles us. But we will sleep upon these and other matters, and talk them over calmly and rationally in the morning; and, as to the nobility of de Mohun's birth, rest assured, that our doubts on that subject can be, and shall be, set at rest by good Master Robert Snelling on his return to the Castle.

As she uttered these words, the fair guardian kissed her fairer ward's lips, and bade her seek that repose which her agitated spirits required.

Prudence closed her casement, drew her curtains, and was speedily undressed, and soliciting the approach of sleep to her harassed mind;

hours, however, passed before she really slept, and then it was but to dream as she slept.

First and foremost, she dreamed that she was again in the cutter; the winds were howling around her, the cordage whistling wildly in her ears, and the waves madly lashing the sides of the groaning vessel, as it lay on its side upon the sands. Again the welcome blaze of the beacon was seen, holding out a hope of safety and of suc-cour. Again did she, by its bright flashes, see the boat upset in its attempts to reach them; and still more clearly, the bold plunge of Hugh de Mohun into the boiling waters, and his vigorous struggles to gain the wreck. Again was she precipitated with him into the waves, and mistrusted his man-ful endeavours to convey her safely to the shore. She felt his warm breath upon her cold cheek, as he chafed her into life again, and repeated her grateful thanks for the preservation of her life.

Anon the vision changed. The well—the burn-ing words of love, poured into her virgin ears, and the awful warning, so mysteriously uttered, were vividly before her—strange, unearthly figures peopled the spot, menacing her with gibbering faces, and amongst them, most conspicuous, the grey woman of Minehead, such in appearance as she had heard her described by the credulous peasantry.

The vision changed again. She was in a strange country—far different in its appearance from her beloved Somersetshire; instead of the lovely valleys, the lofty Tors, and the noble Channel, she beheld a flat, uninteresting scene, on which grew a few stunted willows, beside a narrow sluggish stream. It seemed a picture of desolation; suddenly, however, it became peopled. From two opposite directions, dense bodies of armed men issued—they rushed to the encounter; and, amidst the roar of cannon, and fierce cries of vengeance, the shrieks of the wounded and the groans of the dying came clearly defined upon her ear. Like the figures of the optician's instrument, these melted gradually away, and left two men only standing in the midst of what had been two armies. Foot to foot—hand to hand they stood, striving like demons for each other's life. The bright sparks flew from their swords, as they thrust or cut at each other, and parried the rapidly succeeding blows. At length, one of the combatants fell, and, as his adversary passed his sword through his breast, a white-plumed hat fell from his darkly-clad brows, and disclosed to her the features of Hugh de Mohun. The foe, who wore the livery of the king's enemies, but whose face could not be seen, again raised his arm to repeat the blow. Prudence shrieked out—"Spare him!" and awoke. Ere she could recover her scattered senses entirely, she found Mistress Luttrell by her side, gazing upon her wonderingly and tenderly.

"What ails my child?"

"I did but dream," said Prudence, "I did but dream, and a fearful dream it was;—but it was but a dream, and I will rise immediately."

She tried to fulfil her resolve, but, when she made the attempt, a sickly feeling came over her— her head seemed to reel round and round, she trembled violently, and fell back on her pillow senseless.

Mistress Luttrell, after trying the effect of the usual restoratives for fainting fits, and finding them vain, became alarmed, and dispatched a servant for medical aid. The surgeon, on his arrival, and after due examination of the pulse. pronounced the disorder to be an attack of fever, or of that hideous disease, the small-pox; but he could not tell which.

The rumour that the fair Prudence Everard was seriously, nay dangerously, ill was soon spread about within the Castle and in the town. The last person who heard the report was the one whom it most concerned to learn it. Hugh de Mohun had risen early, and left the Castle for the well of St. Leonard, determined to pass the day by the side of its waters, to see if, perchance, he could solve the mystery of the voice which had pronounced him to be base-born.

CHAPTER XIX.

HUGH de Mohun did not stir from his position beside St. Leonard's Well, until the shades of evening fell gloomily over its waters. He had provided himself with a book and some means of refreshment, in order to enable him to keep his resolve, not to quit the spot until the hour should have arrived, at which the being, earthly or unearthly, had proclaimed him to be base-born, and as such, unworthy of the hand of Prudence Everard.

The hours passed away slowly and silently; no sound was heard, from morning until eve, but the gentle murmurings of the stream, as it trickled from its rock-covered recess into the channel which conveyed it to its destination, and the voices of the birds, as they warbled forth their melodies in the grove.

"I need wait no longer," said Hugh, as he placed his book in his bosom, " but, before I quit this spot, I will betake me to a little distance on the hill, to see if the same appearance will present itself to my eyes, as was seen by Alice and William Luttrell."

Hugh slowly mounted the steep ascent, keeping as nearly as he could, in the path by which the children had descended, which the traces of the footsteps of their ponies pointed out to him. When he reached the summit, he turned round and gazed eagerly at the well.

" By heaven!—but it is strange—well may the ignorant, uneducated peasant deem the mist which shrouds the well to be the wraith of Mistress Leckey! It hath a wondrous similitude to the figure of a grey-clad witch. See it moves its arm and beckons to me: I will not be churlish enough, not to attend its summons."

A few seconds sufficed to bring the active youth

to the spot which he had so recently quitted, and, as he suspected, the nearer he approached it, the fainter the vision grew, and, when he arrived at the well, not a particle of mist was visible.

" That riddle is solved." said Hugh, "the waters and the moist ground, render the air cooler here than elsewhere, and consequently, a vapour, in a state of condensation, hovers over the spot, and is visible at a distance. But the voice?—I would I could solve that mystery as easily."

"What ho! Hillioah! hillioah !" screamed a voice close to the well.

Hugh started, and laid his hand on a pistol which was concealed within his tunic. He looked about him, but no one was to be seen.

" Whoever or whatever you are—appear!"

" Hillioah—hillioah !—Master Hugh—Master Hugh!"

" Whoever calls me, I am here. Come forth, appear!" shouted Hugh greatly excited.

" Here, indeed—I would that you had been there, down at the Castle, and saved my old knees, and my panting lungs so great an exertion ;—dinnerless you have been, and supperless you will be, unless you hasten back to the Castle, where every thing is at sixes and sevens, because forsooth, Mistress Everard is ill and light-headed, and Master Hugh is well and light of foot, and been missing all day, and I forsooth am to be sent, old as I am, because the fools below, have not courage to look upon an old woman in a grey cloak—to search St. Leonard's Well for a straying student."

"How came you hither, Jefferies?" asked Hugh earnestly, of the aged butler.

"On foot, on foot, and a toilsome climb I have had of it. But young Mistress Alice would make me go seek you here; for, as she said, she knows you love to haunt this spot, in spite of the grey woman of Minehead, who is said to haunt it too."

"But I saw you not as you approached, and I was on the hill above," said Hugh.

"Folks must have sharp eyes that can see through a thick mist and a mound of thorns and oaks," said the butler; "but come, your presence is needed at the Castle; for the young Mistress Everard is suffering from your having imprudently detained her in the dews of yester-evening, and is seriously fevered and beside herself."

" Prudence Everard ill! I and away—let us hasten Jefferies, let us hasten, and you can tell me of her ailments as we go along—how, when, where, was she taken ill? speak."

" Nay, if you gallop down hill at so fast a pace, you must needs answer your own questions, for the little breath I have left will not suffice me to run and talk too," said Jefferies.

" Then I will leave you to return at your leisure, and will seek my information from others," said Hugh, as he darted forward and left the old man to follow him as he best could.

He found, from Mistress Luttrell, that Prudence was dangerously ill, and heard from Master Luttrell, that her mind was wandering, and that her thoughts, if they could judge of them by her rambling words, were busied with fears of his exposure to some unpronounced danger, and with some unearthly vision which she had seen at St. Leonard's Well.

Hugh de Mohun was greatly shocked at these

ill-tidings, and grieved to think he should not have heard of her illness before. He fully explained to his friends why he had been absent until so late an hour, and was applauded by both of them for having endeavoured to discover the person who had so wrongfully insulted him, and so cruelly alarmed Miss Everard.

"But the physician—what report does he make? is he skilful? does he give any hopes?" said Hugh eagerly.

"He repeats," said Mistress Luttrell, "that a fever, the result of cold or excitement, or something else, is raging in the veins of my dear ward."

"Is that all the information his skill enables him to give? he must be an ass—an ignorant ass," said Hugh.

"Nay, he is sufficiently skilful for a country mediciner, and shews his wisdom by not assigning any specific cause for his patient's disorder," said Master Luttrell, smiling at Hugh's earnestness.

"But the result? does he give any hopes of a speedy recovery? tell me, dear madam," said Hugh.

"He can only tell us that much depends on the result of the drugs he has administered, and upon the patient being kept perfectly quiet. The morrow, he says, will enable him to speak more positively."

"Dear madam," said Hugh, "had you not better seek further advice? this mediciner is a mere village apothecarv : every moment is of vital consequence, let me mount a horse, and seek further aid."

"You will be puzzled to find it, Hugh, nearer than Taunton, or Bridgewater, but rest assured of this, that, should it be needful, further aid shall be procured. Now to supper—that my lady here may return to watch over the slumbers of. her sick ward."

As Master Luttrell said this, he seated himself at the table, and commenced his evening meal. Mistress Luttrell followed her husband's example, for she had to prepare for a night of watchful sleeplessness. Hugh, who had lost all appetite, in fears for Prudence's safety, thought both of them verv unfeeling persons, for being able to swal-

low food while one so dear to them was lying ill.
He tried to eat, but he could not, his mouth
felt dry and parched. He took the wine-cup
presented to him by Jefferies, and drained it to
the dregs. The draught revived him, and he was
enabled to inquire more calmly into many particulars of which he was still ignorant.

"So, young sir," said Master Luttrell, assuming
a seriousness of brow, as soon as his lady had bidden them farewell for the night, and Jefferies
had placed all that was requisite for their final refreshment, before them, "so, young sir, it seems
that you have contrived, in the space of some three
short weeks—"

"Very short ones—" said Hugh, "I never knew
three weeks pass so speedily."

"Or so happily, I presume; but do not interrupt me. You have contrived, it would appear,
in this very short space of time, to lose your own
heart and gain that of my fair ward in exchange."

"That I have lost my own, I will not deny;
for I cannot, with any show of truth; and I would
gladly know that I had won a heart so pure and

guileless in exchange; but of that fact I have no assurance," said Hugh.

"You have confessed your love to Prudence, did you ask for hers in return? be candid, Hugh de Mohun, you speak to a friend."

"I will be candid. I have confessed my affection to Miss Everard. I would not however demand her hand, until I should have cleared up the mystery of my birth, and ascertained whether my rank and my fortune were worthy of her acceptance. Thus much I had told her, when the mysterious voice forbade our union, under the vile assurance that I was basely born."

"You have, so far, acted well and honourably, Hugh. It will be necessary that the man who weds Prudence should have both station in society and fortune to maintain his rank. She is of unsullied descent, and my duty is to see that no stain be marked upon her escutcheon. She is poor too—nay almost penniless—for her father, the last of the Everards of Luxborough, was entangled in the meshes of the law, and sold his estates to maintain a system of hospitality, which he erroneously deemed essential to the character of a country gentleman."

"Trust you to my honour, sir," said Hugh, proudly, "not to solicit further for the hand of your fair ward, until I find my name to be pure and unsullied, and my fortune adequate to her deserts."

"Both of which points, though doubtful at present, may, as I believe, be solved by my worthy chaplain, Master Robert Snelling, on his return."

"I would that he were here now," said Hugh.

"Time enough—time enough—for, should he solve our doubts favourably, both you and Prudence Everard are too young as yet to form a contract which is to last for life. Should your claim to the unsullied name and the wide domains of the Mohuns be made good, you shall have my consent to aspire to a union with Prudence, after she, should God spare her to us, and yourself, shall have passed three or four years in the world—"

"Three or four years!—an eternity!" said Hugh, looking amazed.

"——in order, that both of you may be sure, that none others have charms enough to make you regret your hasty choice. But stirring times, or I mistake not, are at hand. Hugh de Mohun, in your love-dreams, you have not noted the progress of events in the outer world. The king is daily, nay, hourly threatened; not only his power but his person is in danger. The Church is assailed by men, who, feigning to believe all that her enemies speak against her, are eagerly awaiting an opportunity of possessing themselves of her fair inheritance. In her defence, and in the defence of my lawful sovereign, this arm shall be exerted, and these broad lands, bequeathed to me by my ancestors, shall be willingly sacrificed, to raise and maintain troops, that will fight in their lawful king's behalf, so long as the walls of this my Castle hold together."

"And, should such a necessity arise," said Hugh, "I should feel a pride in ranging myself under your banner. The plume of feathers shall not be plucked from the crest of the Luttrells, while a Mohun can wield a weapon in its defence."

"I believe thee, Hugh, and I thank thee also, nor will I fail to avail myself of your services should they be required. I will now wish thee a good night and refreshing slumbers,—promising you the due fulfilment of my word, with respect to Prudence Everard, on the terms I have mentioned; provided that the report from the lips of good Master Snelling shall be, such as I doubt not it will be, confirmatory of your claims to an unspotted descent and suitable means for its maintenance."

Hugh shook the extended hand of his friend, and retired, but not to rest. He summoned Jefferies to his apartment, and bade him go seek the latest news of Miss Everard's condition. The answer was unfavourable; she was restless and more feverish, and the mediciner was about to take blood from her surcharged veins.

Hugh could not sleep, but threw open the casement of his room, and leaned out of it, as far as he could thrust his body, that the cool night-air might allay the fever, which burned within him, caused by anxiety for the safety of her whom he loved.

"I would," said he, "that Dr. Gravebovs were

in the neighbourhood, for, though a mere Quack-
salver, as he is termed by the professionals, his experience is great, and his drugs have wrought
many and wondrous cures. I marvel where he
may be found; but, if Prudence Everard be not
pronounced out of risk when the morrow's sun
rises, I will seek him; even should I be necessi-
tated to journey as far as the city of Bristol for the
purpose."

For some four or five hours, did the anxious
youth tread his apartment, as the seaman treads
the deck of his vessel in the night watch. Now
and then, he gently opened his door and listened,
if ought might he heard to increase or diminish his fears; all, however, was still—silent as the
grave, on which, for the first time in his life,
he thought sadly and seriously. At length, worn
out with fruitless watching, he flung himself in
his day dress on his bed, and fell into a deep and
heavy slumber.

Vexed and hurt was he when he awoke, to find
the sun already far up in the heavens on his daily
course; and still more vexed, when Jefferies, steal-

thily entered his apartment to tell him that Master Luttrell was awaiting him in the hall.

"Unfeeling wretch, that he must think me, to be slumbering here when, perhaps, death may be—but, Jefferies, I have passed a sleepless night, and, though the mind was wakeful, the body at last failed me," said Hugh, as he sprung from his bed. "But Prudence—Miss Everard—what report bring you of her?"

"She is no worse," said Jefferies.

"Thank God for it," said Hugh. "I will but bathe my temples, and be with you speedily."

When Jefferies had left the room, Hugh de Mohun threw himself on his knees beside his bed, and offered up a prayer for the invalid's safety and recovery; as pure and sincere as ever issued from the heart of man. He then plunged his heated brow into the cool water, and arranged his dress as speedily as possible, and joined the party assembled at the morning meal.

There was one there whom he little expected to see. Julian Bachell was seated beside Mistress Luttrell: he rose upon Hugh's entrance, and

proffered him his hand; Hugh grasped it in silence,
and scarcely raised his eyes to see with what expres-
sion of feature his former friend regarded him, but,
dropping it quickly, sought the side of Mistress
Luttrell, to obtain a confirmation of the aged butler's assurance that Prudence Everard was not worse.

"She is not worse, de Mohun," said Mistress
Luttrell. "She has passed, it is true, a troubled
night, and the fever, in despite of the blood-let-
ting, is not diminished. It is accounted a favourable
symptom that it hath not increased."

"Would it not be well to seek further advice, as
I suggested last evening," said Hugh.

"That is provided for," said Master Luttrell.
"Julian Bachell, having heard from some Dunster
men, of the ill-health of my ward, hath already des-
patched a messenger to Cutcombe, to ensure the
services of an eminent physician of Taunton, who is
still in attendance, at intervals, on the lady of Master
John Pym, who is scarcely as yet convalescent."

Hugh de Mohun looked at Julian Bachell, as if
to ask him how he had dared to interfere in a matter which could not concern him; and fancied that

a smile of triumph passed over his features as he returned his gaze.

But little was spoken during the remainder of the meal, save on subjects of public interest, which had so few charms for Hugh that he scarcely listened to the remarks which were made. As soon as the meal was over, he left the hall, and walked rapidly up to the keep, and looked about, upon the distant hills that stretched away towards Cutcombe, as if to see if the physician who had been summoned so unexpectedly by Julian were on his road to the Castle. No one was to be seen, except some shepherds watching their horned flocks, and Hugh turned away from that quarter in a listless manner, and wandered to and fro on the green turf of the Keep.

In his wanderings, he, without designing it, approached the arch of the ruined tower, and again gazed upon the shields and crest, which Julian had informed him were the arms borne by the Mohuns, who were formerly lords of Dunster and of many fair and broad lands besides.

" Am I entitled to wear those arms as mine by

legitimate descent, or am I not?" said Hugh, aloud ; for he believed himself to be alone, and far from the hearing of any mortal being.

" Not without the bend sinister, the mark of the base-born, being drawn across them," was replied to his question, in the same loud, screaming voice as he had heard on the eventful visit to St. Leonard's Well.

" Who is it that so unhesitatingly answers my doubts?" said Hugh. " Speak—I will listen."

No further reply was made to him, and Hugh, after searching the building and the bushes around it, to see that no one was concealed within reach of him, moved away, saying, " Well, no matter, when Master Snelling returns, I shall know all."

" Ay, *when* he returns, you will know all," screamed out the same voice.

" By Heaven! it came from the ruins! some one lies concealed there: I will find him, if he be mortal, and make him repent of thus rashly taunting and insulting me," said Hugh, as he dashed under the old archway.

The decayed door gave way readily to the weight

of his person, thrown hastily upon it, and Hugh rolled in, amidst a heap of rubbish and clouds of dust, which his violent entrance had produced. His search was long but vain; no one was to be seen.

Slowly did he descend to the Castle, and anxiously did he await in the library the arrival of the Taunton physician: it was late in the day when he arrived. His visit to the sick chamber was a prolonged one; and, when he left it, he frankly stated that the chances of life and death were so nicely balanced, that he could not venture to say which way the scales would turn.

Hugh de Mohun turned sorrowfully away, when he heard what he believed to be a confirmation of his worst fears, and for that, and the succeeding day, knew not how he passed his hours, though the servants knew that he neither ate nor slept, but wandered from room to room, and passage to passage, seeking intelligence of the state of Prudence Everard.

The morning of the Saturday dawned, on which the return of Master Robert Snelling was expected.

Hugh de Mohun had ceased to wish for his return ; for what mattered it to him, whether he could
proclaim him rightful heir to the Mohuns, if she, on
whom he wished to confer their unblemished name
and estates, were to be taken from him ? The mediciner however, announced that a favourable change
had taken place in the night, and that he believed,
that nature had won the battle over disease.

CHAPTER XX.

"MABEL, wench! Mabel, girl!—what ho! Mabel! the devil's in thee—Mabel, I say, come hither, and put things in order, for Master Robert Quirke's reception: that your master is mad there's no question, and your mistress is not far behind him; to think they should go tramping up to Ashley-Combe, merely to see the new-trained bands go through their exercise, under the orders of young Julian Bachell; and Master Robert Quirke, the richest habitant of Minyead, coming to pass his evening, and smoke his pipe at the Ship Aground!" said Master Luckes, the old harbour-master.

"Well I'm a coming, as fast as I can," said Mabel—"I must tidy myself, I suppose, before I can wait on Master Quirke."

" Ay, ay —dress, dress—nothing but dress! but not to please the eye of old Master Quirke. The St. David is expected in harbour this evening, and the folk do say that Master Jenkins's mate, Welsh-man though he be, hath found favour in the eyes of Mistress Mabel. Well, well—to think that my son Richard and his wife should go gadding after a parcel of country loons, in body armour and scull-caps, instead of staying at home to receive the worshipful company of Master Quirke and the Captain of the St. David! And to lock up the buf-fet too, in which the strong waters are kept, when they know that their ale sits but coldly on the stomach ! "

" There is ginger in plenty," said Mabel, " my mistress will not be long ere she returns. The buffet would not be locked, did not some people apply to it so often, when they have free access to it, as to muddle the few brains that nature has provided them with."

" Get thee gone, thou art saucy, wench," said old Master Luckes, "get thee gone, but yet, stop— as thou sayest there is ginger in store, you may make me a cup of warmed ale, and season it with a little spice and some sugar; it will serve me to sip until Master Quirke comes."

"Well, here he is, and in good time," said Mabel, as she showed him in; and as I live, Master Jenkins with him. I will just run and see the St. David made fast to the pier, and be back again to take their orders, as soon as they are ready to give them."

Away scudded the girl, and was soon in the embrace of her lover, the mate of the St. David; a few hurried words assured them that their love was unchanged, and a promise from the mate that he would visit her, as soon as he had made every thing snug on board, enabled Mabel to hurry back to her duties, just as old Master Luckes had called down upon her head every malediction, with which his memory supplied him.

"Nay, be not angry, Master Luckes," said both of the guests; "Mabel is a good girl, and is only gone to greet her sweetheart upon his safe return."

"She is a spy—a vile eaves-dropper and a tale-bearer," said the old harbour-master; "but for her tittle-tattling about my love of the Dutch bottles, I could offer you something better than the cold ale and still colder cider from my son's cellars."

"Provided the ale be good, and sufficiently spiced, it will serve my turn until Master Richard comes back," said Quirke, "so, when Mabel hath had enough talk with her lover, order her to bring us pipes and a warm tankard."

"Nay, an old Master Luckes lacketh patience to await the opening of the buffet, I can give him a dose of as good Scheidam as ever warmed his old nose," said Jenkins, producing from the folds of his large wrapping coat, a bladder containing about two quarts of the liquor the old man loved.

"Ahah—ahab," said the harbour-master, applying his lips to the mouth of the bladder, which was tied to a bit of elder, hollowed out to form a mouth-piece, "ahah! but that is good— I will but taste it again, and then order Mabel to furnish neated water and sugar and—"

"Avast there!—steady, old fellow!" said Master Jenkins, "a bladder holds but little, and if you pull away at it so heartily, you will leave your friends but a smell instead of a taste."

" Ah, I did but put my lips to it," said the old man; "but it hath a glueish quality about it, which makes it hang to one's mouth."

Mabel, who had hurried over her little flirtation, now came in, and furnished the guests with all that they required. They had not long lighted their pipes, and sipped their glasses, ere the host, Richard Luckes, entered, accompanied by Giles Tudball and his mate Will Bowering. Their appearance was heartily greeted by all the party ; for Giles had been absent, inland, for some three weeks, and Will had only returned from a long trip over to Holland, on the day before.

"Let us make a night on it," said Giles, " I have put my old woman in a good humour, by placing a tolerably well laden purse in her hand, and Will's good woman hath such a store of goods to sort and stow away, that she will not miss her husband, should he sit up to hear the cock crowing. I have news too, my masters; news well worth the hearing, and if Master Richard will but send a trustworthy person to Will Bowering's house, he will find there a something, in the shape of a tub of real Nantz, that will help us to pass away the time."

" I will go myself—I will not entrust it to another, for fear of accidents," said the old harbourmaster. " I will but taste it, under Mistress Bowering's eye, to see that no mistake be made, and be back again anon."

" Not so—not so, sit thee still old boy; who would trust a wolf to bring home a lamb, or a kite to carry a chicken to its roost: sit thee still, and be content to have your share of the Nantz, when it shall have been safely conveyed hither."

As Master Jenkins said this, and thrust the old grog-lover back into his seat, the rueful aspect of his face was so ludicrous as to cause a burst of laughter at his expense.

" Were I not an old man and weak to boot, you would not treat me thus, Master Jenkins, you d——d Welsh skipper you; to insinuate and intimate that I would take advantage—unfair advantage—of Giles Tudball's keg! may I be—"

" Over a reeking goblet of its contents," said

Giles Tudball, "as thou shalt be, if—*if*, mind—you conduct yourself quietly and peaceably, as an old man should do."

I did but jest—Master Jenkins knows, I did but jest ; but he is ever fond of trying if my English temper be as hasty as his Welsh disposition is."

"Nay, your blood is naturally cooler than mine I allow," said Master Jenkins ; "but it hath such a quantity of strong waters mingled with it, that it runneth through vein and artery in such a tide, that the cable of your discretion is liable to be parted."

"Ay, like the cable, and a strong one it was too, of the Blossom of Minyead, which was bitten in two by a cod-fish, on the Dogger-bank, in his struggles to get off my hook," said Will Bowering.

"An that be not a lie of the first water—as they speak of diamonds—I know not what is," said Master Quirke.

"I will swear to the truth of it," said Will, "for I saw the fish with mine own eyes. It was at least three yards in length, and had teeth, to the full as long as my fingers."

A loud roar of laughter pacified old Master Luckes, and silenced Will Bowering. The host entered with a jorum of hot grog, the pipes were filled and lighted, and, after a few puffs and a few sips, to enable them to ascertain if the weed and the liquor were really good, Master Quirke begged of Giles Tudball the disclosure of the important news at which he had hinted.

" I have been the long journey," said Giles, "and have seen much, and heard more. Perilous times are at hand, and it behoves us to be on the look-out."

" What does Master John Pym—" began the skipper of the St. David.

" Pym me no Pyms, Master Jenkins; though king Pym, as they call him, be a great man in these parts, he is but one among the many, who are doing their best to dethrone our King and to destroy our Church. In every town and every village through which I have journeyed, I have seen such preparations making for the carrying on of a war, that I cannot but believe both parties are in earnest, and bent on trying their strength in a struggle. I have heard and seen much from both sides; for I travelled with merchandize, and had free admission every where, and, from what I have seen and heard, parties are so nicely balanced that the struggle will be a fearful one."

"But the nobility and gentry," asked Robert Quirke, "surely they take side with their lawful sovereign?"

"In the west, such is the case. The larger towns, and the villages around them have placed themselves under the orders of the gentry, and are arming in defence of the king. As I journeyed London-ward, however, after passing the towns of Newbury and Reading, and the royal residence of Windsor, I could experience a vast difference. Neither gentry nor soldiers were to be seen; but on every heath and common, and in every street and maiket-place, crowds were assembled around preachers, who were instilling into the ears of their hearers a poisonous belief that our king, yielding to the advice of Laud and the bishops, was about to suppress the reformed religion and re-establish popery in its stead. In proof, were adduced the

restoration of stone altars and painted windows in
our churches, the use of credences and the sur-
plice, or 'white' as they call it, in the pulpits,
and an assumption of priestly authority on the
part of the clergy, savouring of the days prior to
the blessed reformation.   As I entered the city—"

"Hast been to London then?" asked Master
Jenkins. "Ay have I, and seen what I grieved
to see. The whole city is armed and in opposition to the king."

"And where is the King?" asked every one.

"In the north—beyond Derby, or, as some say,
at York—and, although the flower of our gentry
and our nobles are rallying around him, it is said,
that he is in sad deficiency of means to pay for
the support of his troops."

"And the Queen—is she yet returned?" asked
Robert Quirke.

"I am grieved to say, that a report is current,
that the vessel, in which she was returning with
ample supplies of money and ammunition from
Holland, has been driven ashore somewhere on the
coast, and she herself and all the moneys and

jewels she brought with her fallen into the hands of her enemies. The navy, it seems, hath sided with the parliament and against its king; but the news of the queen's capture are so uncertain, that I would not have you depend upon them."

"I trust they be not true," said Robert Quirke, "and, upon that my trust, I will give you a toast to drink, Giles; let the glasses be filled to their brims: now then, rise every one, and doff his cap—I give, 'Charles Stuart and his Queen Henrietta, and may their enemies perish as they deserve!'—to the dregs, boys, to the dregs, fancy the liquor the blood of the rebels, and leave not a drop of it, now— The King and the Queen—hurrah!"

Every glass was drained, and every voice exerted to such a degree, that the very cliffs, which impended over the Ship Aground, shook with the shouts which issued from its doors.

"Saw you aught of Master Pym, Giles Tudball?" asked Master Jenkins.

"Ay, that did I," said Giles, laughing; "I put on the guise of a Scotch pedlar, and made my way into his house, though I should have had a difficulty in doing so, had I not furnished myself with the newest tracts, abusive of the bishops and the ritual of the Church."

"Saw you aught of Roger Priver and the preacher, Robert Browne?"

" I both saw them and talked with them; Roger is a great man, and, at the head of some half dozen pikes, escorts his master to the house of Parliament daily. The preacher, too, is established as chaplain to the household, and worrieth them, as they owned, with lengthened prayers and graces; none of which does he conclude, without entreating Heaven to visit upon Master Robert Snelling its heaviest malediction."

" Said they anything of the penalties likely to be imposed on certain parties, who imprisoned Master Pym and his followers, and sunk the carcasses of his horses in the Hone river?" asked Will Bowering.

"Ay, and indeed did they; they talked of the shutting up of certain Dunster men in the prison of Taunton, amongst whom the names of those here present were not forgotten," said Giles Tudball. "But now, as I have given you all my news, it were but courteous in you to satisfv me as to what hath befallen this neighbourhood in my absence. What of the Dunster student— Hugh de Mohun? hath any one seen or heard aught of him?"

"I have seen but little, but heard much," said Robert Quirke. "He hath shut himself up in Dunster, and hath become, as it were, a mere milksop; and all, as they do report, for the love of Mistress Prudence Everard, whom, as you may remember, he saved from the waves, on the e'en of our mad doings at Culbone."

"Ay, and he hath, as it were, been mettymorphied," said Master Richard, the host, who had just returned with his wife. "He hath not quitted the walls of Dunster, or at least its park, but hath, as Basil Chipera told me, been sitting within, looking at the limning of his sweetheart, or wandering with her and the little Luttrells, amid the groves to hear the nightingale's song. It would seem that he were entirely changed, and, instead of the bold, sprightly youth we knew him, has be-

come a mere milksop. While Master Thomas
Luttrell has been arming and training his tenantry,
and his once friend and associate, Julian Bachell,
hath been aiding his father in the same good cause,
our wrestler and stick-player, who defeated Bully
Alloway the butcher, and old Master Castles from
Berkshire, hath become a mere hanger-on upon a
fair girl and a dangler with children."

" Fie—fie, Master Richard," said Quirke,
you know that, during the last few days, the life
of Mistress Everard hath been despaired of, and
that the young Hugh de Mohun hath been nigh
distraught about the cause of her illness, which
Basil Chipera, ere he left home with the parson,
Master Snelling, attributed to certain unholy
visitations from her whom we call the grey woman
of Minyead."

" And whither hath the good Master Snelling
gone, to require the esquirage of the cordwainer,
and his parish-clerk, Basil Chipera?" said Giles.

" To Bristol, as it is said, to procure the print-
ing of certain treatises in defence of him of Canterbury—Laud, who hath need of defenders, seeing

that he is close shut up in the Tower, and threatened to be tried for his life," said Master Quirke.

" To Bristol, said you ? I hope not," said Giles.

" And why so, Master Tudball ?"

" Because I was turned away from that quarter, ere I had passed the town of Chippenham, by a report that a plague was raging there, which was killing its hundreds daily," said Giles.

" Nine hundred thousand died there yesterday, only yesterday," said Will Bowering. "I heard it from good authority in the Channel, from a Bristol pilot, who would not approach nigher the city than the Posset Point."

" Where you expect to go to when you die, I know not, Will," said Master Quirke, laughing; " but if lying will ensure you a place among the tormented, you will not fail of it—you have killed more by some eight hundred thousand, in one day, than the fair city of Bristol holds within its walls."

" Well, well I meant nine thousand, nine thousand, and no less. Our old friend, Dr. Aaron Graveboys, hath saved a million by his medica-

ments ; an he were here, Mistress Prudence Everard
would easily spare Master Hugh de Mohun to
take his pastimes with us again," said Will.

"We have seen the last of him," said Master
Richard Luckes, "call me liar else. Never will
Hugh de Mohun enter these doors more, and make
the roof of this room rattle again with his boisterous laughter. He is lost—become a mere milksop."

"I will not call thee liar, but I am here to re-
fute your words, in one respect. I have entered
your doors; but I cannot make the roof rattle with
my laughter. I am here to seek tidings of Giles
Tudball, to know if he hath seen or heard of
my good tutor, Master Snelling, whose return
was looked for to-day ; or of the mediciner, Doctor Graveboys, whose aid may even yet, be serviceable to the recovery of Mistress Everard."

"Hugh de Mohun!" cried the party, as they
rose from their seats to greet him.

"Yes, Hugh de Mohun, but a changed, an
altered being," said the youth, as he took the hands
extended to him, and shook them heartily. "I

will, however, so far resume my former self as to partake of your cup, while my good friend, Giles here, of whose return I heard by chance, gives me the news he brings."

Giles, reluctantly mentioned the account he had heard of the severity with which the plague was raging at Bristol, and, as he told his ill news, he could not help remarking the great change that had taken place in the manner and bearing of the young man. Instead of the joyous, daring look, which he had used to wear, his face was smileless, his cheeks pale, and his eyes dull and dim. His dress too seemed to be neglected, and his hair, formerly the object of admiration to Mistress Richard Luckes, was altogether uncared for, and hung on his shoulders in disordered profusion.

His presence seemed to cast a damp over the joviality of the party; and, when he rose to leave them, to return to Dunster, every one felt his departure as a relief. Yet no one there present failed to regret that one so young and so gallant, so good and so generous, should be, thus early in life, weighed down by anxiety for the fate of those whom he esteemed and loved.

Hugh de Mohun walked rapidly towards the
Castle, by the beach. He had resolved to travel
to Bristol on the morrow, should no tidings be
heard of his tutor that night, for he was sure that
nothing but illness would detain him and prevent him from being at his post to discharge his
duties in the church.

"I am not wont to desecrate the sabbath by
travelling," said Hugh, "but it is of vital impor-
tance to me to see Master Snelling, and I trust, I
may be forgiven, if I, for once in my life, break
the commandment to keep the sabbath day holy."

"The sin needs not to be committed," said a
deep voice in his ear. "I am here to tell you,
that Master Robert Snelling is no more. He
died two days since, of the plague, in Bristol. He
blessed you ere he died, and seemed to wish to
send you some special message; but his tongue
failed him." In the speaker, Hugh recognised the
mediciner.

Aaron Graveboys had come suddenly upon him,
as he turned into the park of Dunster. A thick
film seemed to pass over his eyes, his brain reeled,

as he thought of the destruction of all his hopes of learning the history of his birth and fortune. He fell to the ground, and would have fallen heavily, had not the mediciner caught him in his arms.

Jansen and his master conveyed him up the slopes to the Castle.

END OF VOL. 1.

This book is given special protection for the reason indicated below:

Autograph
Association
Condition
Cost
Edition
Fine binding
Format

Giftbook
Illustration
Miniature book
✓Original binding or covers
Presentation
Scarcity
Subject

CPSIA information can be obtained
at www.ICGtesting.com
Printed in the USA
LVOW11s0746160218
566856LV00029B/452/P